I0518319

The author

Chris Page was born in Sweden in 1962, and brought up in Gloucestershire in the UK. After living in London and New York, he moved to Osaka in 1989, where he is based to this day.

He is editor of Kansai Scene magazine, works in language education and is a freelance writer published in the UK, Japan and Canada.

By the same author

Weed
A novel available in paperback through Amazon and as an ebook through Kindle and all major ebook outlets.

Sites

http://chris-page.com/
http://weedthenovel.com/
http://untalltales.com/
www.psipook.com

Contact

psipook@psipook.com

Un-Tall Tales

Tales

Collected short fiction and poems by Chris Page

Psipook
Press

Published by Psipook Press

Chris Page has asserted his right to be identified as the author of this work

Published in 2011 by Psipook Press

The stories in this volume were published in an ebook titled *Shorts* in 2009, except 'Dumb Novel' and 'Escapology', which are published here for the first time.

'The Freebie' first appeared in *The London Magazine*, July 2002

www.psipook.com

psipook@psipook.com

ISBN 978-0-9559588-5-4

Cover design by Chris Page

CONTENTS

The Freebie

This story first appeared in the July 2002 edition of The London Magazine

BILLY WAS just thinking he ought to call *The Enemy* when the phone rang. It was *The Enemy*.

'Hi, this Justin Lastname of *The Enemy* here. Can I speak to Billy Freeb?'

The Enemy? Justin Lastname of *The Enemy*? *The* Justin Lastname of *the The Enemy*? Billy was not sure what to make of this. On uncountable occasions in the past howevermany years Billy had not called *The Enemy*. Whenever he was conscious he thought he ought to call *The Enemy*, but he never actually did. Now they were calling him.

'Yeah, this is Billy Freeb,' he said.

'How're you doing Billy?' asked Justin, brightly business like. 'Your name has been buzzing round the office lately. We at *The Enemy* are very excited about what you're doing.'

Billy was picking his nose. He stopped and said 'uh.'

'Yeah, we thought we'd do a short piece on you. Nothing grand just yet, maybe five hundred or a thousand words, a photo. See how it pans out.'

'Ah.'

'If, of course, you agree. What do you think, Billy?'

'Er ... How did you find out about me — my work?' he mumbled at the edifice of awe and fear that had popped up next to the telephone.

'Well I have a big memo right here on my desk, Billy. Makes interesting reading, almost enough for a story but without one crucial thing — you yourself, Billy.'

'I see … As a matter of idle curiosity, do you know why you happen to have a big memo about me on your desk?'

'Oh, I imagine one of our staffers saw one of your gigs and put your name about.'

'I haven't actually done any gigs,' said Billy. 'That's kinda the point, isn't it.'

'Oh …' the sound of a seismic shift of papers, something heavy toppling, 'that's — ' and the light summery rustle of memo, 'right. Well, I suppose one of our staffers didn't see one of the gigs you didn't do and decided to put your name about. So what do you say, Billy? Why don't we meet for lunch? I …'

'Aaaaaaaaaaagh!'

'Billy? Billy? You all right?'

The mention of food had sent Billy into peristalsis.

'Aaaaaagh!' he expanded, but pulling himself together with an eviscerating drag on his cigarette, he arranged to meet Lastname at an Indian restaurant in Islington.

'See you there,' said Billy.

'Check,' said Justin.

Great! Fame! And Billy had done absolutely nothing to earn it but think about it! And a free lunch to boot! Not that he ever ate — that was against his principles, or against the chemicals in his blood — but a free lunch means free booze — and that was very for his principles and the chemicals in his blood, both.

But fame. 'I don't believe it' said Billy lamely, the dead receiver still in his hand. 'Help.' Abandoning the handset

2

to the floor, he lit a cigarette and stumbled giddily from the hall into his room.

He felt profoundly nauseous. His body didn't miss food too much so long as he remained supine or drunk, but he was neither at the moment, and now with this adrenaline rush on top of this morning's quart of black instant coffee and ten Camel, his legs suddenly felt rubbery and he badly needed the toilet.

'I don't believe it. I can't believe it. I refuse to believe it. Someone's yanking my chain.' Either that Lucien Savage had put someone up to it — in which case he was dead meat in the Kropotkin Arms — or the call was genuine, in which case he would have to face an interview with the gargantuan Justin Lastname ... and there from, record contracts, gigs at Wembley, TV spots, fame, wealth, an active and varied life — unlimited sex, drugs — everything he had ever wanted. Really, it was a no-win situation.

The thought of drugs helped to steady his mind.

He had to get rid of this deeply settled sensation of poison and incipient death, get clear-headed, get on top of the situation. He did this by making another pint of black coffee and pacing round his flat drinking, smoking and retching.

He reasoned his next job was to find out whether the call from Justin Lastname was straight up. With this new task he took his pacing into the spare room of his spare, lopsided flat.

The spare room was unused except by himself. He would sleep there once or twice a week when that Lucien Savage squatted Billy's own bedroom, overriding Billy's own squatter's rights in order to do sex in Billy's bed to whomever. That whomever was invariably a very recent whomever whom Savage had just met — perhaps just minutes before — in Billy's neighbourhood, from whom he wished to keep his own proper location a secret and/or whom he couldn't wait the length of time it took to get across town from Stoke Newington to do sex to.

Savage hated Billy because Billy had a two-bedroom squat which he refused to share with anyone, because it was the only squat in the world with a telephone, and because Billy's universally connected parents had found the gaff for him and sent round a council workman with keys and a claw-hammer to open it for him. Billy's parents had done this in the hope of keeping him off their backs and out of their pockets. Indeed, with Billy safely stowed away down here in Hackney they might be able to make that move to Richmond without him finding out where they had gone or even noticing.

Savage would usually show up between one and six in the morning and put upon Billy's sleepy-stoned-drunk head while propping the unconscious whomever against the doorframe. Billy would put his foot down: not this time. Invariably the argument would get round to the flat theme and Savage's line would go like this:

'Listen, man, you've got all this space here which you jealously guard, which you, which you squat like a Tory. You've even got a telephone that you never use, for Christ's sake — I mean what's the point of having a telephone if you never talk to anyone? You're a bloody hermit, Billy, you don't deserve friends. Look, if you won't let anyone live here, why not just be a human being once in a while and let your mates dip a finger in your manna?'

Savage was not rankled because he was without adequate accommodation, having talked himself into an overly generous share of someone else's squat in Kentish Town, and neither did he believe that Billy was taking space that could be better used by any of London's tens of thousands of more deserving people. Savage was rankled simply because he was that kind of guy.

'I'll tell everyone in the Kropotkin that Mummy had your squat cracked for you,' Savage would threaten. Savage knew a lot of things. He was a stockbroker and in order to trade his shares — his cathode blips, his abstracts, his non-products; like an air traffic controller trading radar contacts — it was imperative that he knew an awful lot about different things. Dragnetting for knowledge, he ended up knowing a lot of things that were not strictly relevant to his trade. Thus, for example, he knew that Billy had not come by his squat by the usual ritual of crowbars, Loony Brew, sweats, and cold nights on raw floors. In fact, he knew a lot else about Billy, almost everything in fact. He knew so much about Billy partly because they had grown up together, and partly because he was secretly shagging Billy's mother.

With this Kropotkin threat Billy always gave up arguing. Of course, Savage could simply have said 'Mummy, Kropotkin' as soon as Billy opened the door, sending him to the greasy, malodorous sleeping bag in the spare room without debate, saving everyone a lot of time and precious calories, but that would have been no fun. It was no victory unless you rubbed your opponent's nose in the futility of opposition. For his part, Billy could have surrendered the moment Savage rang the doorbell. However, he was strongly possessed by an optimism derived from an over-active compensatory fantasy function, and this optimism consistently told him, adamantly, without any apparent irony, and without any obvious reference to the unencouraging mountain of precedents, that this time he would fend Savage off.

It was this same mechanism that allowed him to believe that his outward lack of activity was in fact tightly coiled potential.

Billy could call Savage, find out by oblique means
whether he had made the Lastname call. He could address
Savage as Lucien. Savage hated the name Lucien, and
insisted that people call him Savage or, better, Sav,
because Sav was reminiscent of savvy, which kind of
means suss. However, this plan was fraught with danger
and required some careful thought. Hell, he could just call
Justin Lastname at *The Enemy*. That was the only sure way
to find out. Yes, that was what he would do. With that, his
nausea intensified, and without thinking he fled the flat.

A little later, bolstered by a very rapid can of Stupor Brew
and wearing a second in his hand, he made the call
expecting to be greeted with indignation and outrage. Billy
was risking his life with this manoeuvre: one harsh word
could be the end of him and nearly had been on many
occasions. A less than doting word or look from the staff
at the local burger joint where he went for the free smiles
could condemn him to bed on a vodka drip for a whole
week. Instead, after a suitably important time on hold, he
found himself talking to the same Justin Lastname.

'What's up, Billy?'

Once Billy had laboriously explained that the cat he did
not have had mistaken the big dog-eared memo pad on
which he had not written the name and address of the place
they were to meet for the big dog-eared Persian that had
never lived next door — on which Billy's cat would have
certainly had a crush had they both existed — and had
raped the note into illegibility, they reconfirmed the time
and place of their meeting,

'Cheers, Billy. Thanks for calling,' said Justin.

Now Billy's elation was unrestrained. He drained his can
in one, and while he waited beerily by the phone for a
whole two minutes for Savage to call so he could say

'Sorry Lucien, can't make the pub for lunch, I've got to see Justin Lastname about the band,' he reflected that *The Enemy* could not have called at a better time. Yesterday was Giro day and he still had nearly twenty pounds left, and he was at a relative peak both mentally and physically. Then he stumbled into the toilet, threw up and fainted when he tried to stand.

By the time Billy arrived at the restaurant he was in much better shape; he had got himself together.

He had got himself together with an unpretentious but proficient bottle of red — something with Graves on the label — while sitting on the big mausoleum in the middle of Abney Park Cemetery. The fog — like everyone in London, a late riser — laboriously and reluctantly lifted itself off its dense mattress of trees and shrubs and grass and sloped off to find a quiet spot in which to while away the day. Billy toasted the dead, he drank himself normal, and as he did so he even managed to lose the feeling that the Lastname call had placed in him that he had been caught *in flagrante delicto* with a sexual fantasy by the very object of the same.

Striding up Upper Street from the wrong bus stop, soiled wine glass stowed in the pocket of his old overcoat, there was even a spring in his step. The spring came not from his undeniably light spirit, but from the persistent rubberyness of his legs, one or other of which would occasionally spring the wrong way causing him to go down on one knee to make gentlemanly proposals to lamp posts, passers by or clouds. Compared to lying unconscious on the toilet floor, head wedged between bowl and wall and pillowed by a pile of grey, shredded newspaper, he was doing very well indeed.

The restaurant was not crowded but neither was it quiet. A small group of off-duty BT engineers were filling the empty tables and chairs with an overflow of laughter and shouting. They were enjoining one of their band to eat two whole tablespoons of lime pickle on one narrow wedge of papadam. Billy stood inside the door looking for Justin Lastname who was not there.

'A table for one, sir?' inquired a waiter.

'I'm meeting someone,' said Billy. 'I believe we have a reservation.'

'Name?'

'Lastname.'

'That would be helpful, sir.'

'No, the name is Lastname. Lastname is the surname.'

'We don't have Lastname on our list, sir.'

'Er, try Justin.'

'Mr. Justin? No, I'm afraid not.'

'No, Justin's not a last name, it's Lastname's first name. Justin Lastname — that's his full name.'

'And your name, sir?'

'My first name or last name?'

'We do have a reservation in the name of Enemy.'

'That'll be it, sir,' exclaimed Billy, stumbling in his much unused restaurant etiquette. 'I mean ...'

'This way Mr. Enemy,' said the waiter.

Billy took his window seat and ordered a bottle of wine to further calm his nerves.

'Freeb!' said Billy, slapping his head when the waiter left.

He was a little early; it could not be said that the journalist was late. Billy lit a cigarette and composed himself. He wondered whether any of the big men laughing across the restaurant had heard his conversation with the waiter, had heard Lastname mentioned and was impressed. He wondered if any of them had even heard of Justin Lastname. None of them were looking at him in any manner, impressed or otherwise. They were impressed with the lime pickle and were negotiating with the waiter for another bowl, even though they were already sweating quite profusely. Maybe they would be more impressed later when Justin himself, who they would surely recognise from the TV, came in and sat at Billy's table.

On the other hand, Billy mused, maybe the loud men hated music and never ever watched TV. Maybe they spent every spare hour in Indian restaurants drinking lager and making their brains bleed with lime pickle and vindaloo in which case they would have no idea who Justin Lastname was.

If they hated music, they would probably like Billy's.

In a sudden outbreak of affection for everything in the universe, Billy wanted to go over and talk to the men about music. He wanted to tell them that their laughter and the purple veins bulging from their red foreheads were forms of music in themselves. They were happy, they were preoccupied, he left them to it.

Billy's wine had arrived. Lastname had not. It could now be said the journalist was late. He sighed and stifled a gag. He lit another cigarette from the one he had just finished. He drank some wine.

Justin Lastname came in.

Billy stood. They shook hands.

'Billy Freeb.' said Lastname, sounding a little impressed and sizing Billy up. 'How're you doing?'

Billy wondered whether he should say "Nice to meet you".

'What's up,' he said.

The BT curry club fell silent and looked round. They were clearly impressed that Billy was meeting Justin Lastname for lunch. Billy was really very impressed that he was too.

'Let's eat,' said Justin.

Lastname's physical presence confirmed what Billy had suspected: he was a big man. Short and skinny, what he lacked in physical stature he made up for in pandimensionality; he was big in five or six dimensions, maybe more, and when he had parked himself and his other-realm protuberances into a seat, he looked uncomfortably wedged in, far too big for the table or the restaurant. He would have looked more at home reclining on a comet between solar systems thought Billy.

Talking of comets — those eyes! Those eyes that preceded him everywhere! He had brought them with him today — the full pair, the big, too wide, slightly bulging ones that were wild and keen and savvy as a nocturnal predator's. Hyperanimated, Lastname's eyes were like those of an owl that had strayed into a pet shop full of gerbils. Oh yes, feral and hungry, thought Billy, and they had done some things, those eyes. You could see it in them and around them in the taught blast lines that radiated from the craters of their orbits. They had seen some life, they had seen some parties, they had seen some shows. They had put on some shows too, fronted many a show put on by E, C, LSD and ESB. And not just his eyes, his face holistically carried his life, the sum of Justin Lastname (what baggage! Billy traveled light): thrusting assurance in his beaky nose, appetite in his tomato-splat mouth, momentum in the friction-tanned leather of his skin.

No mere manic street preacher, no simple mind, no pretender, he lived by his words. Always more than a man at work, he was kraftwerk, wonder stuff, a blur. The most incisive hack since Brutus's was hailed as a mother of invention, ever provocative and never simply read; he was to musicians everywhere kingmaker, slayer of iffy pops, anthrax to sheep on drugs, airheads, lemonheads and radioheads; the difference between nirvana and pavement. Auteur, proclaimer, mapping the musical swells in living colour, he was a credit to the nation, the hack who can. Take Justin Lastname or take that!

As a result, Lastname was not only the most respected writer for the most respected rock journal in Britain and a presenter of at least all the TV shows for the under twenty-fives, he was a recording star in his own right, had a column in the Sunday Telegraph and had just been paid an undisclosed sum in the upper six-figure range to write a novel he had not even begun to think about yet.

They ordered: samosas, onion bhajias and chicken tikka to get warmed up; vindaloo for Billy, phall for Justin; bindi bhaji, saag bhaji, alur dom, biriani, and pullao for balance; plenty of naan, roti, chupattis, and papadams to fill up on; chutneys chilli, onion and mango, and vinegared chillies for a bit of oomph. On some macho impulse to prove they could eat something that would not actually induce delirium, they asked for raita, and as an afterthought, for the sake of authenticity, dhal. Finally, Billy ordered a bottle of Mindanao-deep St. Emilion ('88) to add some 3D to the spices.

As the waiter skipped away, Lastname placed his pocket tape recorder on the table between them.

There was an expectorant pause. Billy apologised.

'Shall we?' asked Justin with raised eyebrows and a gleam of devilry in his eyes.

Billy assumed an interview posture. He had never been interviewed before but he knew all about it from *The Enemy* and from the TV and it was, in truth, not a wholly unrehearsed move. Moreover, this was just one in a whole repertoire of postures he would be employing this lunchtime. This opener was a very relaxed, very low slouch over his place mat with the glass of wine suspended between thumb and forefinger, hovering near the crown of his head.

'For sure,' said Billy.

With a much-ado flourish, Justin hit the play button on the tape recorder.

'Billy,' began Justin, 'you've kept a very low media profile for a long time. Why break the silence and agree to an interview now?'

Billy thought about this carefully. 'Justin,' he started, 'I haven't kept a low profile for an awfully long time. I've carefully maintained no profile at all. I've kept a zero, a subzero media profile. In fact I've made absolutely no attempt to get my profile in the media at all, nor have I felt any need to project myself publicly,' he lied. In reality, Billy had tried to call *The Enemy* almost everyday in the past howevermany years, but was each time forbidden by his howling, gibbering fear function. Each day, Billy sat on the floor in the hall by the telephone, neutralising his fear centre with napalm strikes of vodka or Loony Brew, or buying its silence with gifts of fine wine or single malt scotch. When he came round, hours or days later, on the floor, curled round the legs of the telephone table, his fear function would be his only still-active faculty. Far from exorcising this little monster, all the years of struggle and alcohol had only strengthened it. The bugger obviously like a drink; so did Billy and they achieved the kind of detente where they agreed to destroy each other indefinitely because they did not like the alternative of not destroying each other. A bit like the Middle East.

But what the hell? *The Enemy* had called him. It was meant to happen.

'I'm breaking radio silence now,' he went on, 'because I've reached a point in my personal and artistic development where it becomes necessary to break that radio silence.'

'Check,' said Lastname. 'So this new openness toward the media is a change in strategy.'

'Not at all. It's merely the one strategy unfolding.'

'Are we going to see a media blitz now?'

Billy did not answer immediately. He changed pose: he straightened, drank, leaned forward with his weight on his elbows, and his forearms neatly folded on the table in front of him overhung by his Tweety Pie rib cage. He made a conscious effort to look absorbed and forgot what the question was.

'Ideas,' he began once he remembered where he was, 'have a life of their own independent of the progenitor. You have an idea and kick it out into the world and you can no longer say "this is my idea". You can say "I gave birth to this idea, spawned this idea", that's OK, you can say that. You can't say this is my idea except in the sense that you had that idea. It's like becoming a parent. If you have a child, it's yours only in the sense that it issued from you, but when it gets to say, seven or eight, it's going out by itself and you don't even know where the hell it is or what it's up to anymore. It's totally got a mind of its own. It has nothing to do with you anymore and to assert possession is an act of denial. Like, my project was conceived way back and since then it's been working as much on its own as I've been working with it. I suppose it must be a strong concept because it's embedded itself in

the human psychic field, replicated itself and finally
manifested itself as a memo on your desk suggesting you
call me.'

'Right,' said Lastname, making notes on his linen napkin,
which may have been questions to ask Billy later or the
first draft of his novel.

'Now, you see, things are that developed, the concept and
myself have entered a dialogue. It learns from me as much
as I learn from it. Progress and development come from
the mutual dynamic interplay which is, by its very nature,
an unpredictable thing.'

'So, ah, you don't know whether you'll be thrusting
yourself into the public eye.'

'Yes, I don't know. I think so, but we'll have to wait and
see.'

The food was arriving. Lastname magicked a bottle of
Tabasco from the ungulate folds of his jacket and began
drooling the red stuff on the different dishes.

'You're putting your head on the editing board here, aren't
you, Billy? Your band, your project is a tad
unconventional. A lot of people are just not going to
understand, are they? You could be exposing yourself to a
degree of public ridicule.'

'That's right, Justin. New ideas, radical ideas, are often
greeted with distrust, hostility and fear ... even destruction.
They used to burn witches, didn't they, and had Jimi
Hendrix been born in the seventeenth century, it would
have been interesting to see what the Witchfinder General
would have made of "Voodoo Chile". As it was, Hendrix
burned his own guitars. A retroactive fear of heterodoxy?
Was he a little afraid of what he was doing? If you spend
all your time breaking ground aren't you going to wonder
once in a while whether there's going to be anything left to
stand on? No, I'm not worried. I'm quite a bit older than

14

most in this business. I'm twenty-four, I've seen this happen a lot already and I think I have some defensive resources.'

'Jimi Hendrix has recently been deified all over again and he's dead.'

'Maybe being dead makes it easier. A god choking to death on his own vomit once may not unduly hurt his career but twice is going to be hard to swallow.'

'So you think of death as a valid career move.'

'Crucial. I've often considered it. Death is the purest form of activity. It's kinda Zen in its unselfconsciousness; engagement is total ... it requires a lot of commitment and there's no room for compromise. I respect that.'

'Look Billy,' said Lastname, addressing an ostrich-sized leg of chicken tikka, the clouds of garlic billowing across the table making Billy's nose hairs stand erect. 'When *The Enemy* comes off the presses every week, I look at it and I think "wow, I wrote all that? I wrote about all those bands in one week? How did I find the time? Where did I find the energy?"'

Billy nodded appreciatively as if he spent all his time doing huge amounts of work too and not languishing in bed wanking. He poured more wine, pulled carefully on his Camel leery of gagging.

'Because there are an awful lot of bands out there, Billy. An awful, awful lot. Hundreds and thousands of bands, all different colours and shapes, some of which are tops, some of which are bollocks. But everybody's in a band, Billy. Everybody. My grandad's in a band. And they're all very, very busy, Billy. Very bloody busy. Except Take That, of course. Take That are packed in refrigerators when they're off duty so they don't go off. But apart from them, everybody's very bloody busy, Billy, working their ends off for music. Why aren't you in a band Billy? Why am I interviewing you?'

Billy half swiveled in his seat to sit side on to his interrogator, twisted back to face him, jabbed a pointy elbow into his own groin, and rested his chin on the heel of his upturned palm. Billy liked this arrangement because with a cigarette in the hand supporting his chin, he could smoke without moving any part of his body but his fingers. He also liked it because in this pose he rather fancied himself as a post-modern version of Rodin's Thinker.

'I have no band: it consists of four people besides myself who I picked at random from the phone book and who I've never met. As far as I know, they don't know each other and don't know they're in a band because I haven't told them. They may even be dead by now.'

'So you're the only one who knows you don't have a band.'

'Wrong. Quite a few people know I don't have a band. But I'm the only one who knows the specifics. That's been a bit of a problem, a bit of a flaw, keeping things from myself, but art can only aspire to perfection. However, it can be said that for some considerable time I was myself unaware that I wasn't in a band. Then one day it occurred to me. I suppose these things happen.'

'I assume then that all the creative input is yours, that you write all the songs.'

'Yes and no, Justin. In that nobody's writing anything, the project is the purest form of composition. Our input is exactly equal. Well, almost ... in that I am to some extent aware that nothing is happening, I suppose things are a little lopsided my way. But I don't dominate and I don't dictate. We all have an equal say in what doesn't happen and what isn't produced. I don't interfere with the creative needs of the other people who aren't in the band with me, I give them as much space and time as they need to do what they feel they have to do artistically. And they don't impose on me at all. It's very egalitarian that way. We're very good about that. It's very pure in that way.'

'But, Billy,' insisted the journalist, dolloping Tabasco onto his okra. 'But, Billy, even Kate Bush writes songs once in a while. Even My Bloody Valentine write songs from time to time, for Christ's sake. No songs, no lig: it's a rule. What gives you the right not to write songs?'

'Well,' said Billy carefully, 'it all depends what you mean by a song, doesn't it. Burt Weedon's guitar book will tell you that a song is verse, chorus, verse, chorus, bridge, chorus, verse, chorus, or whatever, and we all know that's a total load of rubbish. Just listen to John Peel for ten minutes and we learn that Weedon is a stray extraterrestrial.

'Moreover, it's taken as read that music must involve instruments and melody and rhythm and all that, but we don't really think about that assertion very deeply do we. I mean, look at Test Department and Einsturzende Neubaten: suspension units from locomotives, oil drums, sledgehammers, pneumatic drills, bed springs ... they thought about it, they challenged every notion of what music was about. Except one.

'Now look at Philip Glass and John Cage and Stockhausen and Schoenberg: they knew. And in there comes the non-song, non-music. They would sit down at a piano for exactly a minute and thirty-four seconds, or whatever, without playing a note, stand up, bow — and the audience would go mental. George Chest, the Times' music critic threw his underpants on stage after one such performance.'

'My God,' said Justin, 'you mean ...' He allowed a gloop of curry to escape from the roll of chupatti paused halfway to his mouth and splat on the table cloth.

'Yes,' resumed Billy, 'we've gone that one step further. We've done away with the silent piano, we've lifted all time limits on non-compositions. We brainwashed the pianist into forgetting how to play, then sacked him anyway. We burned down the stage and demolished the auditorium. Then we prized all the sliders off the sound deck and dropped them down the toilet.'

'My God,' repeated Lastname urgently, showering food across the table. 'The temerity!'

'As you once said, Justin, all life is rock 'n' roll, all rock 'n' roll is life. It's everywhere, it's in everything. It's a way of looking at things, it's a spirit of absolute engagement, of total involvement with everything you do.'

'Once said? I say it as often as I can at least.'

'When I feel a song coming on, Justin, you know what I do?' Lastname said something encouraging in samosa.

'When I feel a song coming on, do I pick up my guitar? No way! I do the washing up!'

The illustrious Lastname's ears were waggling visibly, which could have been because they liked what they were hearing but could just have easily have been attributable to the chili.

'Or I clean the windows or swab the kitchen floor — '

'You must have a very clean flat, Billy.'

'— or I watch TV, or go for a stroll. Anything I want, man. It's all the same.' He shrugged and waved the flat of his hand at the restaurant to show to show that all the tables and chairs and waiters were the same. 'Or, you know, I might take a shower, have a crap, have a smoke, drink, get out of my head, bonk, read the paper ... anything.'

Ooh, you little liar! Billy never cleaned his flat, never took showers, never read newspapers and never, ever bonked. Billy spent most of his time, whether in creative mode or not, in a delirium of psychotropics and malnourishment.

'Music is creation,' Billy asserted confidently. 'It's the creation and preservation of moments. But the moment is the important thing, not its pickled remains in the song. Songs: sensation, emotion, thought, all collected together, neatly packaged and tied with a price tag and sold to whomever who promptly forgets about it. Look at all the music that's churned out every day, every week, every year. On the radio and the TV alone there's more than a reasonably sane person would want to keep track of, then there's the universe's worth of other stuff that never makes the playlists, still more that never gets recorded, and yet more that never even makes it out of the garage — most of it better than the rubbish that actually makes money.

'Now, how much of last year's output do we remember? How much of it did we hear? How much of it do we want to remember or hear?'

'I heard all of it,' said Lastname, a little surprised.

'All these moments the songwriters have concretised for us ... in the end they mean doodly to us. I mean what kind of spiritually dead goon identifies with the songs of U2 or Sting? It's all just a sound, an ego and a nice line in threads. What about Yes or Simple Minds? A browse through a thesaurus and the music pulls at your heartstrings like a trigonometry lesson does. How many of these moments resemble any moments we've had in our own life?' he said, leaning challengingly across the table at Lastname.

'Bugger all. But — '

'But that's not the point, is it!' finished Billy triumphantly. 'The music, the lyrics, it's all irrelevant, man! It doesn't matter what you do. Music is totally disposable. You write the songs that get you the fifteen minutes on the stage that gets you the interviews and next week it's all forgotten. And the punter is totally hypnotised by all this. It just keeps going on and on — being a fan is a bit like getting into the star's belly with his curry dinner. Great colours, lots of movement, all sorts of exotic stuff — creates the impression there's actually something going on, and creates the illusion that the punters are part of this activity. Meanwhile, they are being digested by the process.

'It's a big wank,' asserted Billy, deftly karate chopping a papadam and not showering fragments over the table at all.

Billy arched back his head and opened the curtain of My Bloody Valentine locks on his face but sprang right back. 'Let's cut through the crap and get to the moment — not somebody else's moment, but your own moment! That's what you are, your own time, your own experience, the nitty-gritty minutiae of each day. When we turn on the stereo or the radio or the TV, we suspend ourselves, we're living by proxy for that time — time created, time packaged for us. The media is prophylactic; it protects us from life. Strip off, get unsafe!'

Billy was getting well into it now and even allowed his carefully arranged arms to flap about a bit of their own accord.

'Make your own moments, revel in the now — your now not somebody else's then. We could be inventing every second of our day, reinventing ourselves with each breath.

'What I've done is dispose of the disposable product. Why even try to preserve what's dead?

'Lets get on with what's important; let's get on with the interviews and the fame. Let's save a lot of time wasted in senseless writing and tiresome touring. Let's get on with the celebrity parties, the ligging and the bonking; let's get on with the filet mignon and champagne breakfasts, the eco-benefits, the flights to New York for lunch, the yoga and the drugs; let's get on with the trashed hotels, the big houses that use as much energy as a town; let's get on with having opinions however trite or muddled or misinformed on every subject from the arcane to the trivial; let's get on with the senseless trips to Bosnia, the adulation, the need, the love ... and the freebies.'

Billy sat back again. Lastname was wiping spilt curry from the tablecloth and catching it in his other hand, which ferried it to his mouth. Billy slugged his wine and went on.

'I have erased the alien distinction between life and art, between corporately appropriated rock 'n' roll and its true, universal, seamless soul. And in so doing I have unshackled the artist!

'Rock 'n' roll will never die! Long live rock 'n' roll!'

'You,' spluttered Lastname, spraying curry sauce back onto the tablecloth he had just wiped it off and pointing at Billy with a brown and yellow finger, 'have created a vast melting pot, a steaming, bubbling, frenetic stew where the distinction between participant and observer is, is, is ... melted — quantum-wise — where the producer and the consumer become one in a fiery cauldron of activity, each tossed and turned, constituted and dissolved and reconstituted again — ' Justin was in copy mode now, and the little tape recorder whirred approvingly '— but a bit different; difference made meaningless in an overheated realm of bifurcation and diced carrots!

'Do you dare test your toe or any other part of you in this mayhem of energy? C'mon strip off, dive in, lose your skin, ma-an! Get served up in a boiling bowl with your middle digit proudly erect! Come ye of little faith, taste and choke: this is not a meal the soul-dead can digest!

'Man,' said Justin shaking his head, chewing hunked meat and waving his stained finger, 'stuff the Sex Pistols, they were dilettantes compared to this.'

Billy shrugged and glugged his wine.

'Tell me, Billy,' gasped Lastname between great sucks of mouth-cooling air, 'do you practise your scales?'

'Uh?'

'Scales, you gotta practise them. There's nothing but scales.'

To give the journalist time to gather himself, Billy went for a lengthy pause. He drained his glass and emptied the last of the bottle into it.

'Another, please,' said Billy, waving the empty at the waiter.

'Are you ready to order?' he was asked.

'What time is it?'

'Two thirty-five,' said the waiter. 'We'd like to close soon.'

Billy looked at the wine bottle he was holding, half raised in mid-wave and back to the waiter, who sympathetically shook his head: not if Billy was not going to eat.

'OK, thanks,' said Billy. He ran the interview through his head another couple of times in truncated form, trying to home in on and hone the rough bits. It did not look like Lastname was going to make it after all.

He looked out the window hoping to see salvation. He just saw fog. Fog was an odd thing to see on a bright and sunny day, but there you are, that's London for you. Billy had the unpopular opinion that London was a foggy city, just as the old films and folk who had never been there would have it. Funny that nobody else in London ever seemed to notice. Here they all were, plying Upper Street in loud shirts and black shades, not bumping into each other at all. All ready to deny fog; having renounced fog, having thoroughly expunged fog. But there the fog was, like grey candyfloss and thick enough to chew. It was weird fog since it seemed to be generated between Billy's ears and seep out of his head to fill the pubs and the clubs and the streets. Billy wondered if there was a drug you take for it.

Now finding his glass drained, his fags spent, the bill before him and a cordon of silent and implacable waiters around him, he figured it was time to leave.

Leaving left Billy well short of dosh. To show Lastname that he knew what he was doing he had ordered a bottle of wine from near the bottom of the list. He had also assumed Lastname would pay.

Yesterday's dole cheque was ragged down to the stub.

He had also been counting on an advance on a record deal to see him through the next two weeks. That may, he mused, have fallen through as of this lunchtime.

However, the wine had left him thirsty, the lunch hour had left him stressed, and he felt that he now deserved a drink. He also needed to sit down. He was walking with a limp — not because he had hurt his leg but because for some time now his exhausted and neglected body had been shutting down nonessential portions of itself in an effort to conserve energy. It had started at the top and worked down. In the last hundred metres it had reluctantly turned off most of Billy's left leg just to keep the right one working. His head and arms dangled uselessly and his torso lolled loosely on top of his pelvis.

Really he needed to lie down. Really he needed a drink. Really he needed to lie down and drink.

Ten minutes later he was in the King's Head on Upper Street with a stoutening pint of Guinness and a packet of Old Holborn.

Billy was just thinking he ought to call *The Enemy* when he heard a loud ringing noise.

Justin Lastname was also enjoying a well-deserved pint. It had been a hell of a morning. At nine he had reeled out of a taxi — the same taxi that was delivering him from last night — and into an interview with that band. Forget the name. Big in the US. Begins with S. Or The. Never mind, he would check later. Except in the course of the interview it came out that the band was not — or claimed not to be — S or The, but that they were that other lot, N or V. In a fit of petulance that impressed even himself, he had screamed that he had come to do a specific job, i.e., interview S or The and if this band were going to bugger him around with existential crises or schizophrenia or whatever, their careers were off both sides of the pond. In the end, the band decided that they could be anyone Justin wished if it meant the interview would go ahead.

Then there had been lunch with that other guy. Monstrously famous. Big everywhere. He was from that band ... something to do with small animals and anuses. Turned out he was completely sober, was funny and made a lot of sense. But Justin could sort that out when he wrote up the interview.

It was on leaving the restaurant that the big, bald bloke in the Hawaiian shirt had swung at this head with the cricket bat. Justin gathered between ducks and swerves that this was the manager of some band he had done a piece on not so long ago. When the waiters from the restaurant had finally formed a large enough pile on the assailant that he could not move, Justin had pointed out with a quick kick to the grollies that if he raved about everyone, people would think he was failing in his job, then hurled himself into the nearest taxi.

There was much more to be done with the day, but right now Justin had created a very loud and invigorating hiatus, right here in the King's Head on Upper Street in which to recoil his energies ready to spring into tonight's bright nova of events. He was listening to a song, a very good song on his iPod. It was so good he wanted to dance right there in the bar, but because he was Justin Lastname, he kept his eyes down on his Telegraph, his face impassive and allowed only his feet to squirm a bit, out of sight, deep in his Reeboks. Here was that good bit where the guitar went GRRRAAAAAAARRRSKREEE CHUGACHUGACHUGA before the band hurled itself once more off the pinnacle of the verse and into the precipice of the chorus without safety net or bungee rope. The band was called the Smarmpits and the mp3 had been given to him by that Lucifer Savage, the Smarmpit's frontman-singer-guitar hero wherever they had been last night. These lads were going far, Lastname would see to that. He was going to meet them this very evening at some place called the Kropotkin Arms, where they were playing and where, he was assured, he would find lots of booze, drugs and sex. Savage was a stockbroker in his day job so he knew all about drugs and money, and therefore music.

Which reminded him. Today he had done someone a favour. He had not interviewed a bloke with no band called Billy Freeb. That had been Savage's idea.

'He's a sort of conceptualist,' Lucifer had explained, a kind of performance artist, if you like, but this performance involves doing absolutely nothing. He believes that everything we do is art, that everything, like, going to the toilet or doing the washing up is an act of self creation, that we're inventing ourselves the whole time. Like, life is rock 'n' roll.'

'Does he make money from this?' Justin had asked, perplexed not just by the concept, but also by the whole external world and much of his internal world, both strobing at him deep in the acid belly of a Dead Dog event somewhere.

'No, he's on the dole.'

'Sounds like a load of bollocks to me.'

'Of course it is.'

'So wha — '

'So the point is you don't have to meet him. You just call him, make the arrangement and don't show up. It's an interview with a non-musician in a non-band — with a non-bloke, really. Look, he's been down in the dumps since, since ... well, since he was born come to think of it. It's like, he's totally frightened of life, he's petrified of getting stuck in, so he makes up all this bullshit to make him feel like he's actually doing something. All you have to do is make a call and he'll be tickled pink. But for God's sake don't actually meet him, he'd be destroyed. Not that he'd show up: that would compromise himself.'

'I still don't get the point,'

'There are two points: if Billy thought *The Enemy* was taking him seriously enough to go along with his concept, he might put off killing himself. Second, if you do this the E's on me tomorrow night.'

'What's his number?'

How easy, thought Justin, to save a life and spread a bit of light and happiness in this frantic world. Yeah, this world is full of good blokes, mainly me.

Justin was feeling really good, well on top. Lastname was a winner, he was a bright star, a beacon of hope in London's foggy maze. And his effulgence intensified in the wasted presence of that sap across the bar now being carried out by paramedics, apparently dead, leaving behind only a pint of Guinness and a packet of Old Holborn as monuments to his passing.

(2000)

Poems

Underpants and Teeth

every day, day after day after day,
we wash our teeth and
change our underpants

and we wash our teeth and change our underpants
day after day after day

and this is life; this is what we do
to keep the days going by
day after day after day
we wash our teeth and
change our underpants

and we learned from our parents
who day after day after day
washed their teeth and changed their underpants

the need to wash our teeth and change our underpants

day after day after day

and in our turn we'll teach our children

to wash their teeth and change their underpants

day after day after day

and we will go on

day after day after day

washing our teeth and changing our underpants

until we have no more teeth to wash

and no more underpants to change

and then we'll die

and then we'll be dead

day after day after day

Monument

Things could be better,
Things could be worse,
Things could be
if they already weren't

And that chicken died for us

And that chicken died for us.

And that chicken died for us.

And that chicken died for us.

beak all pecked out, wings burst free in a glory of
angeldom, nothing left on the inside but sage and onion,
nothing left on the outside but teeth and forks and obtuse
children who ate the flesh of the chicken that died for us
and left the husks of the insensible carrots

and that chicken died for us, all squawking and clutterfuck
so that we may, and it was a messy rotten business with a
grotesquerie of roasties and a ghoulish slathering of gravy
and severed heads of broccoli, for Christ's sake, we had to
send the children out of the room

dipped a bloodied claw in the gene pool: children carried
on a conveyor to a better place of strip lighting and tv in
the kitchen and popupmicrowavethreespeedblenders and
gastric enzymes. Oh, go to work on a soul

Old Mother Hubbard dying in a palaver of chains and
knives, sudden flashes of no inspiration of no insight, tin
lamps swinging on more chains, and the wine was Chilean
and quite palatable, and death had lots of dominion; death
had lots and lots of dominion

Old Mother Hubbard stripped naked in the glare — from left on the shelf to hung out to dry in the time it takes to snap a vertebra — pumped and primed and taken away from the mounds of chicken shit and the perplexing cycle of too-fast days and antibiotics to protect her from her neighbours

And that chicken died for us, silly bitch.

And that chicken died for us, silly bitch.

And that chicken died for us, silly bitch.

Cats Die

'What's the difference between melancholy and sad, Dad?'

'Hmm. I am sad because my cat died. I am melancholy because all cats die eventually. Sad is pretty quick, but melancholy goes on and on and on.'

Rory and Tanya, five and seven years old, sprawled across the sofa and his lap, were quiet a moment, perhaps trying to fathom the subtle distinction their father had just alerted them to, or perhaps trying to locate some melancholy within themselves.

If the latter, they won't find any, they are simply too new for melancholy. Melancholy is for silly old losers like their father.

H and the kids are having a rare five minutes together and they are reading a book about another melancholy old loser called Joe, who has lost his cat up a tree.

For H, for anyone, it is tough at the age of thirty-nine to accept that you are a silly old loser. The understanding can seriously spoil your life. But H is resourceful; he can deal with it. In fact, he plans to take it lying down.

H is horrified by the utter predictability of Joe's story. Joe dotes on his cat. But the darn thing took a stroll up this tree hours ago and can't get back down again. It is way up there, near the top and Joe is way down here at the bottom. The cat sits up there all on its own, quite unbothered by its predicament, fat and smug and very aloof.

A neighbour comes along with a ladder and offers to help, but Joe refuses because he doesn't want to put the neighbour out. The neighbour tells Joe he would love to get the cat out of the tree because it is such a fine animal and no man should be separated from his cat. Joe says no. The neighbour goes away. Then the fire brigade comes along but again Joe refuses help because he thinks a whole fire engine and crew and mechanical ladder is too much palaver for one silly cat even if the fire brigade is specifically there to help people. The fire brigade goes away. Next the local human pyramid team comes along and say they would love to make a human pyramid tall enough to fetch the cat down. They insist that building human pyramids is their absolute favourite thing and it would be no trouble at all. Joe doesn't want to be responsible for anyone falling off the pyramid or being hit by a low flying jet. The human pyramid team goes on its way.

Along comes a snotty-nosed boy with a catapult, who tells Joe he is such a good shot he can ping the branch with a stone and the cat will drop out of the tree and into Joe's hands. Joe is horrified. Suppose the boy accidentally hits the cat, suppose he did hit the branch but Joe missed the falling animal, suppose the boy missed the tree altogether and the stone pinged on someone's head. So the deadeye, snotty-nosed little dick goes on his way too, leaving Joe to stare forlornly at the cat, no closer to getting his hands on it, his flow of opportunities apparently all dried up.

It was not clear to H what or who Joe was waiting for.

As he was reading, H's mind was elsewhere speculating on the ending of the story. Joe will do nothing useful and will continue to refuse all offers of help. Eventually a big wind will come along and the cat will be blown out of the tree and into Joe's grateful and relieved hands. Then, of course, in the same wind the tree will topple, impaling Joe and his cat with its spiky branches.

'Did your cat die, Dad?' asked Rory, throwing H with this abrupt return to the theme of sad and melancholy.

'Yes, it did, young man. Very much so.'

'When did it die?' Tanya wanted to know.

'Years and years ago. Or was it years and years and years ago? I forget which.'

'Did you cry?'

'What do you think?'

'I think you cried like a poof.' They giggled cruelly.

H was not sure whether he was more put out by the barbaric stereotyping in the remark or by the emphatic dismissal of crying as a legitimate response to nature. Tears, after all, are the wine of melancholy.

'Can we have a cat, Dad?'

'Nope.'

'Why not?'

Why not? Well, cats die, don't they.

'I know where we can get a cat,' Rory announced, inadvertently throwing one among the chickens cooped up in his father's head.

'There's a bunch of kittens of the garden of that old house where nobody lives,' Tanya went on. 'They must have been very naughty because their mummy has left them out there with no food.'

H felt tears at the back of his eyes scratching to get out.

Rori corrected his sister. 'They weren't naughty, just stupid. They keep their eyes closed and they keep falling over and bumping into things. And they are very noisy. If we did that, Mummy would put us in the bushes too.'

'If they stay there, will they die?' Tanya wanted to know.

'I'm sorry, kids. I don't do cats. I do picture frames.' And schoolgirls. 'Someone else can rescue them.' It is H that needs rescue.

'H?'

H was convulsed by the sensation of steel talons scraping down a blackboard deep in his soul: his wife was speaking to him.

'I'm nearly ready. Could you get the kids in the car for me, please?'

He un-gritted his teeth to acknowledge her and to motivate Rory and Tanya toward their coats and shoes.

H now regularly suffered this involuntary reaction of pain or repulsion when his wife addressed him. He didn't dislike his wife — indeed he had always loved her. There was nothing terrible about his wife: she was one of life's cool people, and he would be the first to acknowledge this, albeit somewhat mutteringly. There was nothing hostile in the way she spoke, she was always very reasonable, she merely sounded like a woman who was energetically juggling an active family life, a part time job, a burgeoning career as a painter and a parallel burgeoning career as a rising star in the Labour party. H suffered so at hearing his wife's voice because of everything she was and everything he was not. H was an administration officer with Haringey Council and he had a second career as a maker of wonky picture frames, but that was semi-stalled at the moment; as a career it was pretty non-burgeoning. H was a man swept to one side, ambitions overwhelmed in the wash of the juggernaut that he had married ten years previously. He just couldn't work with all that going on, with all his wife going on.

And that was the other thing. She was always so bloody right. How was it that someone could be so unfalteringly, unerringly correct all the time?

Here is a sample from a conversation that very morning.

Mrs. H had shown the temerity to ask H to do something with the kids for five minutes while she got herself sorted to go out. They were in the bedroom. Mrs. H was getting dressed and H was finding any excuse he could to stay in the room and ogle. It was all very fascinating in a frustrating sort of way to see all those layers of silky and cottony under things go on — Mrs. H had always been very good at silky and cottony under things. That was one of the reasons he had married her. It used to be a lot of fun taking them all off. Now they seemed to go on to keep him out.

H protested at the burden she wished to place on him.

'Look, love. I'm on my way to an important Framer's Guild event and I really have to get ready. This could be my big break. You know, from side job to career. There'll be big painters there, painter's agents, buyers from the major trendy shops. The whole thing.'

This was nothing new to Mrs. H, she had heard it all before. She had suggested he get involved with the event in the first place. Incidentally, H was lying through his teeth. He was hoping to be on his way to a secret assignation with a schoolgirl. He was planning to do his framing networking only on the second day of the event, tomorrow. Adultery with an eighteen-year-old was his plan for today and his overarching plan for dealing with melancholy.

'Making the corners of your frames square would be a big break in your career. Whatever happened to craftsmanship?'

'I know, I'll read a book with the kids,' said H in a u-turn that would qualify him for high office. 'You had better get ready to go out.'

'You're very good. Great imagination. Unorthodox. Everyone gives you that. Very original, all those colours and stains and charred bits, montage — puns even. No one else in the world does that with picture frames. But to say you are going after the alternative market when the real fact is you can't make a square joint to save your life is a cop out.'

'I won't see the kids till tomorrow and then barely,' said H decisively, edging toward the door.

'And anyway, H, what about the bits in the middle? You used to be a darn good painter. Weird, but good — and better than me. It's like one day you went into retreat from reality, gave up painting and everything else and now you are only concerned with the bits around the edges.'

'The edges of reality? The last stop before insanity? Oh, very good. I've been accused of many things in my life but this is a first for lunacy.'

'I didn't say you were mad, you daft sod. I meant you were going to disappear off the face of the world. Or perhaps disappear up your own arse, but my metaphor isn't as flexible as the corner joints on your frames.'

'Oh, thank you. Artistic assassination and psychoanalysis at 10am on a Saturday, which happens to be a very important Saturday. Now, I really must get ready. I mean, do something with the kids.'

'And you're not wearing that shirt are you.'

'Well, just at the moment I am.'

'It has egg stains down the front from where you dribbled your breakfast. You don't want to go to your frame

40

maker's convention with egg on your shirt. No one will want to take your wobbly joints seriously.'

'Thank you, darling. I'll just go bury the shirt in the garden and myself with it.'

H caught up with the kids and replaced their shoes on the correct feet and unbuttoned the coats they had put on so that he could button them up correctly, while Tanya beat him petulantly with a small pink rabbit. Then his wife arrived in the hallway plucking her flapping coat and bags out of the air and taming them onto her body. Mrs. H never simply walked down the hall, she swarmed and flew down the hall — as a flight of Valkyries might. The Valkyries told him about their plans on their way out the door — 'I'll pick the kids up from Nana's so you can get pissed with the framing fraternity and if you get home before me, there's veggie cutlets and plastic cheese in the fridge and harissa-type dressing if you make it' — failed to peck him on the cheek and were gone, the old car chortling down the street toward the main road.

Mrs. H, the ultimately active, ultimately competent woman was off, leaving her husband standing in her turbulent wake, marveling at his wife's seamless and rapid transition from one place and activity to the next. House to hall to car to work, or housework to painting to door-stepping for the local MP to teaching the children French as they got ready for bed, all in one sweeping, rapid, complex gesture. It was the sweeping, rapid, complex gesture of a life going very well indeed.

H had no sweeping gestures beyond dislodging dandruff from his collar.

Once upon a time, the lack of substance to his life was a

source of bother to him. It bothered him into insomnia, chest pains and all sorts of bottles. Then he got fed up with caring. He got wise to it and realised how counter productive caring was. Care and H parted company. H was a busy man in his own realm now: not caring took an awful lot of time and effort and concentration. As a purposive activity, not caring had become for H an open-ended and absorbing process not unlike whittling.

He plodded reflexively down the stairs and into his basement studio-den-computer room. The room was stacked with unfinished frames, half-read books and abandoned canvases; this was his space, his domain, the sandy hole where he kept his head. Whenever he was alone — quite often given his wife's unstill lifestyle — he would hide in here and look at the naughty pages on the internet and commune with his cyber-flirts. His wife thought he spent all his spare time working on the imaginative and colourful picture frames for which he ought to be famed. He was not working when she was not at home, he was engaged in passive-aggressive rebellion with pornography.

The computer was on and there was email. It was from Helen. He was alarmed. Helen was not just one of his cyber flirts, Helen was an extraordinary flirt, and she was going to rescue him from his own life and she was going to do it that very afternoon. However, last night half sloshed on a cheap Chilean wine, he had written to her with a particular request ahead of meeting today and regretted it as soon as he clicked the send button: that would be the end of this bit of fun, Helen would back off immediately. What a prat H was, how clichéd, how old man could you get?

>*You soppy sod! Of course I will wear my school uniform. I think it is endearing that you are so frank about your foibles. Will you bring your Zimmer frame? :-D*

Adrenalin surged and H's heart nearly skidded off the road. Not only was she unfazed by the request, she though it was cute.

H disapproved of pornography for all the best reasons. However, none of the best reasons were good enough to actually stop him looking at the stuff. He made a Faustian pact with hypocrisy, which would let him pretend to be a moral and well-balanced person while his soul burned in a hell of self-loathing. This was a fair exchange since the alternative was missing out on all these spectacularly bare bottoms. And what the hell? His current muffled existence was a foretaste of the ultimate muffling of the grave. No porn, no real sex, no nothing when we get there.

Two years ago, on his new Dell and his first connection to the web, after tasting for the first time the forbidden cyber fruit in a tangible cloud of late-night alcohol fumes, he became abandoned to his fate of sad old man peering at teen arse as some kind of palliative to the banality of his own existence. So he let himself be led through the online id as if he had no control over the mouse, found in his powerlessness and obsession cause for more of the melancholy that had led him to this state, and suffered the occasional tossed cookies.

He haunted the teen and adult chat rooms and the singles rooms and the lonely heart rooms and flirted and talked dirty and was mostly bored by the poverty of, the predictability of, the sexual imaginations he came across. This was yet more grist for his mill of melancholy. One day he found himself chatting privately to this Helen.

The chatting escalated.

>Thanks for the photo. When I opened the mail I dropped

coffee on myself. I've had a woody since. Can't walk.

Three days crippled, three days of priapism, three days of awkward questions from wife, children, friends and colleagues about why H was doubled over at the terminal in the basement with a big agonised smile on his face; three days of Googling images of Margaret Thatcher to douse the conflagration.

>Coffee flavoured woody … Yum! I'll be right over.

>You're doing my head in. I'm an old man. I'm not used to this. I'm fragile.

>Good. You'll be nice and boiling when I get my hands on you. Should be fun.

H was nice and hot now, bubbling and boiling and steaming right there in his chair.

>Why are you interested in an old git like me? My body is a calamity in slow motion. I have a spotty retina, I can't stand without groaning, my willy dribbles like an idiot, my heart hammers to be let out at the first sign of an incline, my teeth won't stay in my mouth. You could have any young stud you wanted.

>The guys at school are all mutant acne monsters. Plus they are all crap lovers

All?

who just think about getting themselves off and then go bragging to their mates about it. Christ, I'm so bored with them! Old blokes are gross, but the ones in between like you are cute. Older men know what they are doing.

And I'm just fed up. There's nothing but A-level bollocks and sensible careers and doing the right thing. All I can see is a living death. The suburbs are like a big cemetery. I want to live but all I get is putting up with crap.

And anyway, you're funny in a goofy kind of way. You say some amusingly inane things. You're cool. You're an artist.

Yes, indeed. H was a maker of wonky picture frames, when he wasn't being an admin officer for Haringey council.

H as the older and hopefully wiser of the two parties might have asked her what crap an 18-year-old in a stable, affluent household in a stable, affluent society had to put up with, but instead he told her about all the crap he had to put up with, his own stability and affluence notwithstanding.

>Whatever I feel about the wife, you know I can't leave the kids.

>I know. Who the hell wants to get bogged down in relationships? No offence. I just want to shag — lots — and have a laugh.

Just like a bloke. The perfect woman. Why didn't they make women like her in his day?

So it really was the big green light for this afternoon. He was about to cross over to the dark side. He was also pointed at what promised to be the most exciting afternoon of his life. How did he feel? He felt hmm, that is how he felt. Definitely hmm. Hmm in this case was a hmm of determination and no kind of hmm of either randiness or excitement. Odd that.

He also felt unready. He needed his phone, some money and some condoms. How many condoms did he need for one afternoon? A whole jumbo box? Just one? Perhaps he did not need any at all, perhaps these youngsters today are able to simply turn off their ovaries at will. Perhaps she could only conceive in season. He did not know. He was out of touch.

He plodded back up the stairs to the bedroom and stripped to change. He had this oversized Gap shirt that was like an artist's smock and ideal for impressing teenage girls and the picture framing fraternity alike. Or it could be the comfy man's sackcloth. Whatever, undressed, he now found himself staring at his reflection in the bedroom mirror.

When much younger he would gaze at his body with some awe. These days he gazed on his body with lots of horror. As he changed from pre-pubescent beanpole into post-pubescent beanpole there was hope and possibility in this body. It was a white, blank slate — or stick — on which a robust, muscular, tanned, dynamic future would be carved. However, the long anticipated upper body development was a full upper body implosion and the debris was tumbling out of his belly. His stomach muscles had all the grace of a half-full shopping bag.

He was supposed to be getting naked with someone this afternoon, sharing bodies with an eighteen-year-old somebody whose belly was sure to be flat and taught enough to roll pastry on and whose upper body development could make a grown man cry. He had seen her upper body development in photos she had sent as email attachments and had indeed cried. He had blubbed himself into a black lake of despair before he had decided to take the matter of upper body development into his own hands, so to speak.

Quick, no time to lose! He had about two hours and forty minutes to turn himself into a young hunk.

He dropped to the carpet in his shorts to testingly do a few push-ups. Having failed the test he worked on his stomach by laying on his back and panting for five minutes, then there was more arm work as he levered himself into a full recline. H regretted giving up smoking when the kids came along because as a smoker he would have had an excuse for being this much of a physical mess.

The reason he could no longer cope with push ups, he reasoned, was all the weight — the weight of all the years in his past, the weight of all thirty-nine of his years. They pinned him down; the years lay like dark heavy blankets on him. Light, air, feeling were all whumped out of him with each birthday as a new blanket landed on top of the pile.

H but dimly perceived his family through the fuzzy mass. He didn't think he had real feelings for them or anyone else or anything else. Not even the schoolgirl he was to meet this afternoon.

Could he remember a time when everything was not muffled in this way? He tried to remember being young. Youth is a time of clarity, a bewilderment of feelings, and sensations. There, surely, resides authentic feeling, something to succour him on his way to the grave. Yet even those memories were vague and remote and the property of another person entirely. Youth was the other side of those damn blankets, on the outside, in the sun and the air with the butterflies and the ice cream vans. H was seeing life through a blanket darkly.

If the imminence of death, the eminence of death, were not enough, this disassociation from his own memories and experience were good reasons to meet the girl today. He rolled over again and this time on all fours tried some pelvic thrusts. These went better than the push-ups. He still had one or two pelvis-thrusting muscles left. So long as he could finish both himself and her in three to five thrusts, all would be OK.

H groaned at the awful predictability of everything: he was like a cliché in a crap fiction: mid life was creeping up on him, he was unfulfilled at work and at home and had developed an unhealthy interest in teenage girls. Bollocks.

He idly picked up his organiser and flipped it open and randomly hopped from page to page. His assignation with Helen was not noted, only the Framer's Guild event. There was not much noted in the book at all. In amongst the blank space there were a few meetings, the odd football match, the occasional petty deadline.

The year as represented in this book was bleak. It was an arid vista of dried stalks, cracked earth and bleached skulls — as were all the years before this. Nothing flourished here, in the present. So all that life behind him amounted to what? The past, it seems, is a barren soil.

H has a building sense of dread that this is it, that despite all the expectations and hopes for something special, this is what his life is; this is all that his life is.

It was not only H. The same dreary entropy was evident in his peers: the suicides, the divorces, the alcoholism, the psychoses, the lonely and the blandly normal; all slaves to inertia; all living in a litter of dreams, hopes, ambitions, and enthusiasms that have been sloughed off like immature skin.

The real sinker, the real killer, the alligator in this swamp of melancholy, is Mrs. H demonstrating on a daily basis, right in his face, that with focus and effort and a pliant, soft sod of a spouse, a meaningful existence was indeed possible.

Flowers decay, cats die and Spurs never win anything. How melancholy is that?

Abandoning the nicely carpeted bedroom floor of despair, H set about making himself presentable for his date.

There was a nasty moment that nearly threw the whole mission out. But H survived it. Just.

A few doors up from his own home, his headlong flight into adultery was arrested by the sound of the mewling of kittens. They were, as Rory and Tanya had told him, in the shrubs in front of an empty house.

H grit his teeth. Someone will do something about it. Someone will do something about it. He was busy. He was on his way to an important framer's guild event. His career depended on it. He grit his teeth, and walked on, hating everyone in the street for not taking care of the kittens for him and hating the kittens for being abandoned.

Suspended between the light and the dark in a grey zone

between the underground and the open air, between past and future, between faithfulness and adultery, H tramps the Escheresque carousel of tunnels of King's Cross station, trying to remember which exit he needs. The sun flashes at him from the top of the street stairs as if it is following him and trying to catch him to say something to him.

He finds his exit and ascends to the street, in front of the station with St. Pancras Road behind him. This is exactly where he is going to meet Helen. The sun is on his face and suddenly everything is a little over-bright and dazzling. He pushes into the milling crowd and sees the girl in the same moment she sees him. H breaks eye contact immediately, scans the newsstands and the station signs and the ground for somewhere to put his eyes. He looks at his watch, tut-tuts like Mr. Bean and leaps onto a number 73 bus, just because it is there and is beginning to move away.

He flops with exaggerated casualness into a seat, still keeping up the pretence of being someone or something other than himself. He can see Helen from his seat although he tries hard not to. She is still standing outside the station and is staring at him with a mixture of confusion and hurt. In the flesh, she is even more gorgeous than in her photos. Slim, medium height, shoulder length straw-coloured hair, and creamy skin. Her eyes are feline — something she shares with Mrs. H. Mr. H had not noticed that before. And Helen is indeed wearing her school uniform — on a Saturday. That must take some explaining.

His heart collapsed to the floor of his ribcage and sobbed inconsolably.

Yet he simultaneously felt elation: he had reached out and grabbed something, but he wasn't sure what. The decision to transgress had removed the need to transgress and he had come back to life. He had saved himself, he had pulled up short of betraying his wife and children and the last traces of a person he had wanted to be. He was the lemming that had turned away from the cliff.

He felt bad for Helen but her disappointment was not of the order of the mistake they had been about to collaborate in. He would text her and email her and sort it out.

H, it transpired, had things to do; he was suddenly a man with a mission. With excruciating serendipity the bus he was on was taking him right to the exhibition centre in Islington where the brethren of frame makers was congregating and where he had an unattended stand.

He got home well after eleven that evening. It was a toss up whether he was more intoxicated by the twelve pints of lager he had wolfed with his fellow frame makers or by his newly recovered joie de vivre. Whichever the case, he was extremely happy.

Mrs H was still up and in the kitchen smoking one of her very occasional cigarettes. It was unusual and absolutely against her own rules that she was smoking in the house but H didn't care. He was in love again. Not specifically with his wife, and not particularly with the bare-breasted teen in the murky self-portraits. H was in love with just about everything regardless and inclusively of it being animal, mineral, vegetable or ineffable — he was coming home from the toppest of all possible top days.

To demonstrate this, and by way of preamble to unloading the full skinny on his remarkable day at the convention — but not mentioning his remarkable five minutes at King's Cross — he danced and shimmied and frugged around his impassive wife until he could get his hands on the open bottle of wine on the counter behind her. He wasn't quite drunk enough to kiss her, but two-stepped elegantly with the bottle into optimum glass-clinking range.

'Cheers', he declared. 'I've had the toppest of all possible top days. Whoa!'

She didn't clink glasses with him, but she did drink a little from her own.

'I was a hit! I was the hittest of all possible hits,' he announced with yet more exaggerated pelvic action.

'They loved my stuff. Loved it, and then adored it — and then loved it all over again.

'This Japanese company Gomi — all very better-taste-than-thou, apparently, but big, big market the buyer told me. He was English so we didn't have to bow or anything. He wants my stuff. Lots of it. Tons of it. I'm going to be big in Japan,' he said with ironic rock star pose.

'Boat loads,' he insisted still trying to get across to his impassive wine sipping, cig sucking wife. 'They are going to buy as much as I can make.'

'One a month?' asked Mrs. H with an icy cruelty that H, on many years of practice, filtered out.

'Now, this Gomi thing is diff. I mean, here's a real wedge-in-the-hand contract. I might be able to give up the bastard day job!' He faked a seizure and backward topple.

'And wait for this: Bones — Bones of Islington, no less — Bones are gagging for it. Gagging! You can see it in their eyes. Not as many units as Gomi, but both ends of the world covered in one afternoon! Not bad, or what? How not-bad-or-what is that, I ask!'

'H, I am leaving you and taking the children with me,' said Mrs. H.

52

'Do what?' H was pumped but he was far from primed. He might have asked her whether this was a cruel joke, but one look confirmed to H that her dial was preset to Not Joking.

The twelve pints of lager in his belly sloshed uncomfortably as his world turned slowly upside down. The furniture slid to one end of the kitchen before plummeting to the ceiling. He sloshed a little wine onto the Habitat floor tiles.

Mrs. H was leaving to move in with Tom Redwood.

'Tom Redwood?'

Tom Redwood. He was the Labour Party North London area coordinator and they had been moving toward this for some time. Tom was ambitious, he was focused, he was hardworking, positive and energetic. He had his own PR consultancy and lots of contacts at Millbank and in Parliament. He was a lot more fun than H, made a lot more money with or without a Gomi contract, and had a bigger willy. They would move into a new home in Hampstead as soon as the purchase was finalised which might be as late as sometime next week. You know how tedious these things are.

Mrs. H regretted the short notice of the end of their marriage and the complete and total out-of-the-blueness of the announcement, but, well, H was a waste of space, wasn't he. A well-meaning, semi-reliable, and honest waste of space to be sure, but a complete waste of space nonetheless. H had squandered his artistic talents in quasi-existential angst, and blamed her for hogging all the action and keeping him down, which was galling to say the least since she did everything with a handicap of children clinging to her legs trying to keep them out of the way for him to work. She had not seen him with a brush or hammer in his hand for months. What did he do in his studio, the basement, all those hours? Did he masturbate at internet porn? That would explain why he never came near her.

H had his good points. He was quite endearing with the children in an awkward, off-handed sort of way and he did say some amusingly inane things when drunk, but Tom was different. The children had already accepted him after playing in the park together — amazing how quickly they hit it off — he was a more positive role model, and he did these totally amazing Teletubbies impressions that everyone loved.

So thank you for the last ten years. It was better to adjust things now they were still flexible and despite the lateness of the hour and his obvious advanced state of intoxication it would be better if he stayed from now in the spare room, at least until the new place with Tom was sorted out. Mrs. H had put fresh linen on the bed already.

Oh, and if he is going to get self-pityingly drunk could be please be sure to vomit accurately in the toilet bowl and not poo anywhere.

Mrs. H was off to bed. She was bushed.

H did what any real man would after being so comprehensively razed and demolished. He summoned whatever dignity he could and left home directly. He left home directly via another bottle of wine and whatever scotch and brandy he could wring out of the Christmas bottles in the dining room.

His mind was reeling like a Weeble hacked in the goolies, and alone with the booze and his shock, H found he was bursting with questions:

What have I done to deserve this?

What have I done to deserve this?

What have I done to deserve this?

There was, of course only one possible answer:

Nothing.

And that was his problem. It was H's nothing measured against Tom Redwood's lots of thing. Tom Redwood: groomed, mobile, sexy, New Labour; over paid, over rated and leg over the wife. H thought hard about his predicament because suddenly he found it didn't surprise him in the least. H wanted to see how much he could think about it without suffering the smallest iota of surprise. It was, after all, so predictable it was a wonder the wife had even bothered to tell him. It was a wonder that months ago he had not just packed up his old navy kit bag and moved into a cardboard box in King's Cross.

Dawn flagged the sky like a priority email as H dragged his old navy kit bag up the street and away from home.

He was not, he had decided, going to move into a cardboard box in King's Cross. It was a tough decision, but in the end he had talked himself out of it. In truth, he was not sure where he was going, only that it was not King's Cross. And he knew he had his Gomi and Bones contracts.

He was pulled up by the sound of the abandoned kittens. Oh no, not cats. Bollocks to cats. Cats he didn't need right now. Yet he knew what was going to happen next.

Peering into the bushes he could just about make out three of them, tottering and blind and mewling, pleading with an implacable world.

He balanced his kit bag on its end against the wall, opened

the top and rearranged the contents to make a nest, then carefully scooped the weightless kittens up and into it.

Now hugging his kit bag, he carried on down the road, silently cursing the awful predictability of everything.

(2002)

Dumb novel

From childhood he had entertained only one ambition, which was to write dumb fiction. As an adult he sat up late at night in his cluttered and cosy writer's den when the kids were asleep and worked on his vocation.

In the day, he would send his dumb short stories and dumb novels to agents, publishers and magazines. And they would send them back with form letters or little slips of paper saying 'No thanks'.

In all the years he wrote dumb fiction he had not sold a single thing. He had published precisely nothing. He couldn't give the stuff away.

Tonight, he is as usual sitting at his keyboard, but instead of writing he is reflecting. He is doing this more and more these days. He is reflecting that he is past 40, he has predicated his whole life on being a reasonably successful writer (not even a runaway success) of dumb fiction, and while he has boxes and boxes of the stuff he is feeling a mite dejected. This is how his life is shaping up — sitting up night after night with his cups of cocoa writing stuff that no one wants to read. It is not as if he wanted to be another Marquez or even another Crichton. He just wanted to get by, writing fun, unpretentious stories that would raise a smile for the reader and pay enough to keep him and his family in the manner to which they were accustomed. That's why he called it 'dumb fiction'. It was meant to be entertaining. Nothing more. It was the kind of stuff in which someone was sure catch his willy in the zipper of his trousers.

Now in the dead of night, with internet radio wafting classical music's greatest hits at him, he fetches from the shelf what he estimates to be about 200 pages of blank paper. These he slips into his printer and prints them all numbered one to 200. Nothing else; just page numbers. He arranges the blank numbered pages in front of him on the desk and wonders whether he ought to give them a title.

Dumb might be good.

Or *Wordless*.

How about *Breathless*?

Just *Less*? No, he was stretching now.

What about *Man Dressed Entirely in White in an Empty Art Gallery*? Now there was a title.

But the pile of numbered pages didn't need a title so he went on to the next thing.

He typed and printed a cover page, which was entirely blank save for a note at the bottom:

'A novel by' — and he put his name and address as he usually did.

Now the cover letter.

> *Dear Sir or Madam:*
>
> *I have had since I was a child only one ambition, which is to write dumb fiction.*
>
> *Here is my first truly dumb novel.*
>
> *Yours faithfully, etc.*

Next he chose at random the name of an agent from the Writers' and Artists' Yearbook, typed up a big envelope, an SAE and the rest of it, and went to bed.

The next day he took his package to the post office, saw it off and then went on to his office job and forgot about it.

That evening when the wife and the kids were finally asleep, he was back at his desk writing the dumb fiction that no one would want to publish, as he was the night after that, and the night after that, and for a number of weeks and months after that. And in that time he sent off a whole lot of dumb stories and what have you, that no one would want to publish and received back a whole lot of notes that said in different ways 'No thanks'.

Over breakfast each day, he would open the letters of rejection — the letters of dejection, he secretly called them — and returned manuscripts, and after breakfast would store the day's pile of negatives in a large cardboard box he kept for the purpose, before going off to his office job.

On one particular morning, one of the letters of rejection was a letter of acceptance — or rather a letter inviting him to lunch, which in publishing circles was pretty much the same thing.

The letter said 'we are very much struck by your novel , which we feel is a powerful and original work.' There was no mention of the name of the novel, just that blank space in the middle of the sentence. He had sent out so much stuff over the years, looking at the name of the agent didn't help him identify which story they were talking about.

At the risk of being late for work, he ran up the stairs to his writer's den and booted up the computer. He located the cover letter he had written all those months ago and had a hallucinatory moment in which he recalled the pile of blank numbered pages and tried to match it with the lunch invitation.

There must have been some bizarre mistake. It seems that

someone in the agency had mistaken the pile of blank pages for a powerful and original work. What a cock up!

Sending the pile of blank pages, his dumb novel — no words, dumb, geddit? — had been an impulsive act of self satire and a minor gesture of petulance inspired by his huge collection of rejections, his advancing age and the rest of it.

There was only one thing he could do — he accepted the lunch invitation.

On the day of the lunch, he took leave from his office job, dressed smartly and stuffed into a satchel some of his favourite manuscripts — ones with actual words on them. He could show them to the agent once they had cleared up the misunderstanding over the blank novel.

In the event, it turned out there had been no misunderstanding about the blank novel. The agents — there were two of them, a husband and wife team — were very nice and without a trace of irony or mockery said they were very impressed with the pile of blank pages, which they had brought along. The dumb novel lay on the edge of the table next to their extraordinarily tasty lunch, looking very riffled and well thumbed. They used lots of words like 'post modern' and 'courageous' and 'brilliant' and 'concept' and 'art' and there was at least one reference to André Breton.

He was dumfounded. He had no idea whether to explain why he had sent the pile of blank paper, he had no idea whether to bring up the other manuscripts, the ones that had actual words on them, and in the end said nothing much at all.

The three of them agreed to move ahead with talks and agreed to meet again another day at the agents' Bloomsbury office.

He got home in the afternoon a little muzzy with wine and

the circumstance of being taken seriously for a little joke, and wondering how he would explain this odd predicament to his wife, who would surely be aghast that after all those years of sacrificing normality and a sensible career to writing, he was getting acknowledged for a completely blank pile of paper.

He waited for the kids to go to bed before he said anything. They were sitting cosily on the sofa, the television was off, she listened with great interest to his tale and at the end was very impressed.

'You clever so and so!' she said, staring into his eyes and stroking his hair.

'Don't you think I should tell them how it came about, why I did it?'

'Why not? Your Dumb Novel' — it had now acquired caps in the way they spoke of it — 'works on so many different levels.' So he did tell the agents about the novel's genesis. But before that, he and his wife made love on the sofa, which was something they hadn't done in a long time. He then went to bed without doing any writing, which was something else he hadn't done in a long time.

He told the agents in their office over a copy of the contract, which was lying on the desk between them, and after necking a very stiff whisky they had put in his hand.

After a moment of silent reflection the woman said, 'Isn't that a lovely story. You know, your Dumb Novel works on so many different levels.'

'Absolutely,' said the man. 'I think we might be able to make use of that story in the promotion. Cheers!'

And they had another drink and signed the contract.

Yikes! thought the author. *Blimey!* and *Wow! Golly!* and *Gosh!* There was now no need to have reservations or feel guilt. Everything was out in the open. Clearly he was being offered real money for a pile of blank pages that he had sent off on a complicated but not very worthy impulse.

Fine.

They had yet more drinks and he was introduced to a whole lot of new people who kept popping into office, usually staying for a drink or two before popping out again — marketing people, publishers' reps, graphic designers, production controllers, major authors, partners in the company, literary critics, the man from the off license with some more bottles, and so on.

That night for the second time he went to bed without doing any writing. He didn't have to, he joked. That was the kind of writer he was.

In bed he felt like he was glowing in the dark. He was a real writer with a contract and a large advance though he was yet to publish a single word he had written.

But really, was the pile of blank paper so bad? He thought about it at length and felt happy and proud. He liked his pile of blank papers. Everyone did.

He liked the passage that went:

And he also liked this bit:

But his absolute favourite part was:

His dumb novel was published before long. It was the quickest editing and production process the agents had ever been involved in, they told him with some pride.

There was quite a lot of hype about the publication of he book. There was for example a press conference at which he was not permitted to speak. There was book signing at which he sat behind a white screen unseen by the people who came to see him. People were hired to march around the streets with blank white sandwich boards. Completely blank advertisements went up on the busses and all over the tube.

The book itself had, of course, an entirely blank cover with just the words 'A novel by' — and then his name.

The broadsheet reviewers loved the book to bits. It sold in truck loads. *The New Yorker* requested an extract, and got one, pages 27-35. On his way home from work one evening he saw a woman reading it on the underground. She was turning the pages very slowly and deliberately and running her eyes and fingers over each one before turning to the next. He didn't really know what to make of this but he accepted it, as he did the first sales figures and royalty cheques.

His writer's den suddenly filled with light. This was because he was now able to give up his office job to stay home and write all day. It was a dream come true.

He set to writing with a new vigour, and the stuff he wrote was just as dumb as the stuff he wrote before, which is what he had always liked, but which didn't have a very good track record. Something was changing now. When he looked at his dumb fiction it seemed wooden, trite, inauthentic. All his output now looked like that. None of it bore any resemblance to the sublime quality of his blank book. Nothing in common at all. His dumb fiction and the Dumb Novel could have been written by different people.

Now he felt truly like a failure. Here he was, the writer of the kind of dumb fiction in which the main character would get his penis caught in his trouser zipper, feted as a post-modern master on the strength of one petulant little joke and quite unable to follow up with anything real.

He summoned all his courage and took some of his manuscripts to see his agents.

The husband and wife agents looked over his stories and passed them back and forth between themselves with wooden smiles fixed on their faces, rather in the way an uncle and aunt would regard some detailed portraits of cat poo created by their favourite nephew.

'Ah!' exclaimed the woman with sudden insight. 'Early

work!'

'Early work!' chimed in the husband with obvious relief.

'Lovely,' they both intoned in a sort of syncopation.

'My, how you've grown,' laughed the woman self-consciously, and handed back his manuscripts.

'Let's keep these to ourselves,' said the husband.

Back home, the creator of these-we-must-keep-to-ourselves got thoroughly drunk. That gave him an idea. He speed wrote a novel while completely inebriated. It was wild, it was ambitious, it was huge, it was sprawling, it was uninhibited. It was like a literary roller coaster and it was rubbish.

He wrote another which was the history of mankind as told by a dwarf who had spent his life locked in a trunk and sealed in a basement in Rumania. It was an instant early work.

He then wrote a novel about the evil that people do in a babble of random foreign words culled from all the languages in the world with the help of online translators. This turned out to be, when he showed it to his agents, something else to keep between themselves.

One afternoon, in another moment of his ever-more frequent drunken episodes, he collected up approximately 250 pages of blank paper, which he numbered using his printer and sent off to his agents immediately and by express delivery.

He didn't have a chance to regret this particular impulse because he was woken out of his hangover the next morning by a phone call from his agents exclaiming that he had another hit on his hands.

He went through the rigmarole again of contracts and

launch parties and press conferences at which he wore a gag or was draped with a sheet and had to put up with universal adulation.

Surely this new blank novel was a repeat of the last blank novel. Not a bit of it! The critics were very much taken with the fact that it had twenty-five percent more blank pages than the first one, and mentioned this fact as often as they could.

The author spent increasing amounts of time sitting in his writing den staring blankly at the keyboard of his computer — and increasing amounts of time in his cups.

His wife worried, his friends fretted, his agents grew anxious that he might not produce another bestseller.

Eventually, in the middle of yet another fruitless afternoon, in his torpor and his stupor, he decided that enough was enough. He renounced writing. He gave up on his long-cherished desire to write dumb fiction, or any kind of fiction, come to that. He was going to retire as a writer — no, not even that. He was not a writer, he was a compiler of blank pages, whatever that was. He was quite simply going to go back to his office job, if they would take him back.

They would take him back. Not only would they take him back, but they would take him back into the position he left, which had just become vacant again. He was going to slot right back in where he was before. What a relief it was to put all that pressure and palaver behind him. Maybe he would take up gardening. Or learning Esperanto. Or painting garden gnomes.

He did give up drinking.

On the day he was to start back at his old job he leaped out of bed at 6:30 as was his custom, clear headed, refreshed, and feeling as light and happy as he had felt since all the silliness had started with that first pile of blank pages. He threw open the curtains and then threw them closed again. Summoning his most trepidatious manner he peeked out the curtains again: his front garden and the street outside were full of reporters. Reporters with microphones and recorders, reporters with notebooks, reporters with cameras and zoom lenses and aluminium step ladders, reporters with camera crews and vans and satellite dishes. Apparently, he was under media seige.

In a panic he booted up his computer and went to the online news services where he found himself looking at the front of his own house through the lenses that were arrayed outside. He saw himself throw open the curtains and then throw them closed again. He saw his cat sitting on the front doorstep waiting to come in for its breakfast.

Best selling author throws up literary life for humble office job, said one headline.

Dumb Novel author seeks the reclusive life, said another.

Writer turns back on fame and riches for office desk, they went on.

The broadsheets made approving comparisons between him and JD Salinger and Thomas Pynchon.

Some articles speculated that he may be taking an ordinary job to research a new novel or that going back to an ordinary job might be another piece of absurdist performance art, a sort of dumb novel in motion. And they all wanted to know from him what he was up to and deluged him questions the second he opened the front door to let the cat in. As the animal trotted in, tail high and showing its anus to the journos, it gave its master a reproachful look as if to ask what the hell he thought he was doing bringing all those clowns to the house.

Meanwhile, none of the journalists guessed that he was giving up writing because no one was publishing anything he wrote and that he had more self respect than to spend the rest of his life playing a silly game only the agents and critics seemed to understand.

It was this self-respect that made him determined that he would not be intimidated from going to work. He dressed and got ready in the usual manner, and ate a sensible if rather hurried breakfast. When he was ready to leave he slipped on a hooded windcheater, a peaked cap and a pair of sunglasses as a sort of disguise. Then he hefted his bicycle, which he kept in the front hall, onto his shoulder and phoned an immediate neighbour to whom he apologised and of whom he asked a small favour.

Then he took his bike through the house to the back garden where his neighbour helped him climb over the adjoining garden wall. Then it was through his neighbour's house and out the front door as if he lived there. However, the press pack instantly saw through his ruse and were upon him as if he was the last ever news story in history.

Rather than racing down the road as he planned he sort of weaved and wobbled his way through the reporters, ignoring their questions but saying, absurdly, 'Mind out the way! Mind out the way!' That was the only comment the press got from him all day even though they pursued him all the way to his office. 'Mind out the way!'

His boss behaved as there wasn't a braying press pack in his car park, said how glad he was to have his ex-employee back, and just got on with things.

At the end of the day, the ex-author struggled through the press all the way home. He was not inconsiderably miffed about all the unwanted attention when he was just trying to normalise his life, so, having no better idea, he decided to call his agents —his ex-agents — to complain.

There was no answer from their office, and he eventually tracked down the lady agent on her mobile. She explained tearfully that she was at her husband's bedside at the hospital. He had suffered an accident.

'Oh no! How awful!'

At first she didn't want to say exactly what happened and the ex-writer didn't want to pry, but just as he was about to wind up the call she volunteered the information that was too awful to bear alone. Her husband had caught his penis in the zipper of his trousers.

After a few days when all he did was get on his bicycle, go to work and come home again, the press got bored with hanging around and found something else to do with their time. His agent came out of hospital suffering no permanent disability and life got back to normal. Kind of.

He would go to work every day as he did before all the nonsense about his blank books, but in the evening when the children had gone to bed he would sit in the living room reading something, or listening to music or talking to his wife.

One evening he put down the novel he was reading and stared thoughtfully at the wall. He still couldn't decide whether to take up gardening or Esperanto or painting garden gnomes.

He placed a bookmark in the novel, put it down, went up the stairs to his cosy writing den and booted up his computer. He put his hands to the keyboard and with the enthusiasm of one finding a long lost friend took up writing his dumb fiction right where he had left off.

(2006)

Escapology

One

He had himself chained, bound, straitjacketed, locked in a trunk that was similarly chained, welded shut and dropped from a helicopter through a hole in the arctic ice cap. On international TV.

He vanished all right. No one saw him again alive or dead.

Boxing Clever

As he was chained and placed in the trunk he knew he had no escape plan.

However, he had said he would do it and everyone was so excited about it, how could he back out now? Besides, everyone was watching, which was nice and flattering. It showed they cared.

He was sure he would figure out the trick to escaping once he was in the box. The understanding would come to him when it was needed.

After all, lots of other people had done it.

Houdini made a living out of it.

Right now, he would just let things progress.

My Loyal Body

The water streams into the box through a flaw in the welding at one end. I expect an air pocket will form at one end of the trunk when the pressure of the water and the air equalise. Unfortunately I am upside down as the box plummets into the deeps of the Arctic Ocean and the air pocket will benefit only my feet.

My body is kicking and writhing and struggling to keep me alive. My body is loyally going down with a fight – this body that has stayed with me since I was born, this body that has grown up with me and kept me going without me having to really think about it and when other bodies weren't much interested in me; this body of a little boy in the form of a man.

My loyal body. I am flattered at the effort it is going to on my behalf.

The least I can do is think of some way out of these shackles I have placed on my body, and then think of some way out of this box. But at the moment I really don't have a clue, and the frantic efforts of my body, quite independent of my will are quite fascinating, even distracting.

(2004)

Bog

Adapted from the weblog of the same name

September 27, 2008

I am baffled by the number of ads I get in my email for penis enlargement pills and therapies. I am baffled because I enlarge my penis almost every day and it is very simple. All you need to enlarge your penis is an erection. When you have an erection your penis gets bigger and turns the other way up. It can inflate to about six times its normal size. Not bad, I reckon, and no expensive drugs involved.

Yes, a simple erection will rapidly enlarge my penis to a handy size, if you'll pardon the choice of words, and is in a state where I can use it in a number of different ways. I can use it, for example, as a substitute banana if the fruit bowl is looking depleted. It makes a useful plunger for clearing blocked sinks. You can prop open windows with it and make tents. If you should find yourself in a riot, you can use it as a baton. It's also quite convenient for cleaning the wax out of the ears of elephants.

An erection has the advantage of speed and portability. If you order pills, you have to get out the credit card and wait for about two weeks for them to arrive, if they ever do. An erection you can have straight away with only the slightest manual effort.

And of course, if you don't have a penis of your own, you

can borrow mine.

Definitely sausages for tea today.

May 3, 2006

I had sex today. Not a lot of sex, just a bit. Well, it turned out there wasn't that much in the bag.

It was packaged in that slightly deceptive way that suggested you were going to get a biggish portion, but when you get the wrapping open you find that it's mostly air inside.

At least the bag had SEX in big letters on the side. That's how I knew what I was getting.

Because of the sex, there was no need for sausages at teatime today.

April 17, 2006

I must be sure to nurture the little Tamagotchi in my soul.

Feb 17, 2005

Dear Blog,

Those voices in my head are speaking to me of sex with fish. Of course, a fish is a Freudian image of a post-coital penis. And a halibut is a Freudian image of a post-coital penis that has been run over by a bus.

The voices also talk of Republicans as if tormenting me with memories of the demise of Picasso's halibut. During the Spanish Civil War, the fish was confronted by Franco himself. George Bush is, of course, a close personal clone of General Franco. Franco demanded of the fish 'Are you a Republican?' and the fish stared back at him with those fishy, unblinking eyes and flexed its gills a little, which is, of course, fish speak for 'No way, José'.

'You can't fool me by denying it! I know you're not a Republican, you slippy, slappy thing!' barked the General and had the halibut promptly shot.

'You will shoot this progressive halibut promptly at the eleventh hour. And don't be late.'

And so it came to pass that Picasso painted his massive Fishist monument to the horror of being on time for anything, known to posterity and all those who turned up later as Halibut. The name halibut is of course significant for being the Spanish word for halibut. Sadly the painting was blown to smithereens in the Fascist air raid on

Guernica.

With those ghosts exorcised, sleep well, sweet blog.

September 4, 2004

I noticed today that the trees are covered in twigs and leaves. That's what comes from being outside all the time. The council should invent a tree brush and tidy them up a bit.

Sausages for tea.

September 3, 2004

I saw a cloud today.

Sausages for tea.

May 27, 2004

How many uses for a banana are there? I can think of a few.

- *mimikaki* for people with large ears

- if tied to the bottom of feet they are a cheap alternative to roller blades by virtue of the slippy quality of banana skins
- a crutch for a small person
- a device for cleaning around the U-bend in toilets
- a neck support for passengers on long haul flights
- a stirrer for your tea
- a friend to talk to
- using advanced laser technology, a banana could be a device for storing huge amounts of information such as a novel like War and Peace: using clever mathematical formula you can encode War and Peace as a single long number: using clever laser technology you measure the exact mid point of the banana, then convert your number code for W&P to a fraction of one, and burn a line exactly that fraction of a centimetre from the mid point of a banana, and voila, you have the entire contents of W&P stored on a banana
- a non-returning boomerang
- a dug-out canoe for mice
- an artificial *chonmage*
- a lump in your pocket
- prosthetic fingers for amputees
- a snorkel for people who don't do their snorkelling under water
- vegetarian sausages

May 223, 2004

Of all the stupid things people say, one of the most stupid is 'Would you like a nice cup of tea?' I mean, what is the word nice doing in that sentence? It's the sort of thing daft old grannies like to say. 'Ooh! Let's have a nice cup of tea.'

So I went round to my Gran's the other day and I said, 'How're you doing Gran?' and she said, 'All right, you know, considering.'

She's dead, my Gran, but she takes great care of herself, you know what I mean?

So she says 'Come in, sit down. Would you like a nice cup of tea?'

I thought to myself, *God, if I hear that one more time ...* But I said, 'No thanks, Gran I'm all right.'

Then she said, 'Would you like a horrible cup of tea?'

I thought for a moment. 'How horrible? Without sugar?'

'Without sugar. And I'll spit in it.'

'Nah, I'm not too bothered, thanks, Gran.'

'I'll put some spiders in. No sugar, spit, and spiders. And I'll make it with toilet water.'

'Aye, all right then. Cheers.'

'And how about some nuclear radiation?

'Nuclear radiation?'

'Nuclear radiation. I'm got some yellow cake.'

'Now you're talking, Gran. Champion!'

January 3, 2004

A disturbed night. A New Age coven decided to take over the house, and some aliens decided to occupy one of the bedrooms.

The house filled up with coven paraphernalia and coven people. The aliens had squatted one of the bedrooms to set up a bar — it was nothing to do with the coven and was merely an added inconvenience. These particular aliens set up their bars whenever and wherever they please. The bar was supposed to be a nighttime thing only and they were supposed to move on. The aliens were bright pink and had four or perhaps six legs. I watched them drinking. They would take one swig of their alien booze and spring from the bar stool to the wall to which they attached themselves feet first to pass the rest of the night in wide-eyed catatonia. As the evening passed the wall became covered in this staring, stoned aliens. Apparently alien booze is very good.

The pink bar tender thing assured me that they would all be off the wall and out of the house by morning. I was sceptical.

Escaping the bar, I found that spare space in the house, and seemingly the closets too, was filling up with sleeping small people. Apparently these were a smaller version of the human race, perfect in every respect. Idealised creatures, an idealised alternative to humanity — the good of humanity in essence? They were being collected and sheltered (stored?) by the coven. They were a coven project.

They're filling the house with homunculi and elves, I complained.

Next thing, a coven member had cornered me and was trying to explain their worldview. So I am in the middle of a house full of sleeping New Age super beings and stoned pink aliens, arguing metaphysics with a zealous old biddy. I try countering her with the apophenic argument, that religion is merely the desire to invent an order to rationalise away apparent disorder or inexplicableness; that there is a sufficiency of order and meaning in the universe and that don't need to invent silly religions to make sense of everything. It was evident that the woman had no interest in opening her mind to reason and thought I was being bloody-minded and hostile for not accepting her view. She pursed her lips as if dealing with a naughty and wilful child and the argument petered out.

Sausages for breakfast.

November 21, 2003

On my way to work this morning I was reading Haruki Murakami's Wind Up Bird Chronicle. I don't know if you've read this novel, but if you have you will know that it has some pretty frank sex scenes in it and I came on one of these scenes while hanging from my commuter handle. It's weird. The book has 605 pages and just a few of these sex episodes, but I only come on the sex when I am on the train. What do you make of that? I don't come on these scenes when I am alone or in private. I come on them when I am on a crowded train, standing crushed between smelly old men and old women who look like sacks of potatoes. Anyway, so I'm reading this steamy scene this morning and I guess I was in a pretty vulnerable state because I started to overheat, if you know what I mean. Right there, with all the commuters and the bad breath, I am getting a woody. So I stop reading and look around the carriage to find something to distract myself before it gets too obvious. And I make eye contact with this young woman right in front of me. I figure she had noticed my state of heated fluster but instead of being shocked or offended, instead of mocking me, she was getting pretty turned on too. I mean, it was just obvious. So we stared at each other, each with the same thing in mind. She was pretty darned good looking too. So this is a situation. We are two strangers consumed by the hots for each other — I mean urgent hots — but we are on this crowded train. What to do? Without a word, we climbed up on to the luggage rack and had energetic, wonderful sex right there, above the oblivious heads of the other commuters who were perusing their morning papers, listening to walkmans, reading books, staring out the windows, scratching their balls, picking their noses. Eventually the train reached my stop. She pulled on her clothes and got off the train too. Most people were getting off here. On the platform I looked for her, but she had been absorbed already in the thick crowds. Absorbed, dissolved. Gone. And me too. I went on my way to work.

October 10, 2003

In my fridge I have a pack of "100% natural cheese". I scoured the supermarket for "100% unnatural cheese", but I couldn't find any. I expect they had sold out.

October 4, 2003

I went to see a film. It happens.

I sat down in the auditorium with my pop and my popcorn and I looked around at the place. I opened one of the beers I had smuggled in which I was saving for the start of the film.

I waited. And I looked around and I ate and drank. I like

pop and popcorn and smuggled beer. I like pop and popcorn and smuggled beer because they're good.

I waited quite a while and, you know, the more I waited the more I looked forward to the film. It was going to be really good. I could tell. I had decided. It was going to be like a film made by Terry Gilliam, David Lynch and Stephen Frears all together. Only better.

So I waited and I opened another can of beer and went and bought some more popcorn and the anticipation got kind of unbearable, you know. It was just too exciting.

And I wondered when the film would start. I could have just asked someone or looked at my ticket stub or whatever but I was actually enjoying the popcorn and the beer and the sense of imminent adventure so I didn't get round to it.

Eventually, I opened another beer and snuggled down in my seat a bit further and I wondered where all the people were anyway. I was the only one there. Like, they were going to miss the start of the film. I suddenly thought there might be some kind of mix up over theatres. But if all those other people were just going to sit there in the wrong theatre waiting for a film that wasn't going to happen, it wasn't my problem. Why should I risk missing the start of the flick just to go and find them?

So I waited some more and wished the film would hurry up and start. I don't know how long I can just sit here.

There's only so long they will allow it. They generally throw you out after seventy or eighty years.

Still, I'll give it a little longer. After sitting here so long, surely the film is about to start.

September 15, 2003

I am not well read. I have not, for example read the New York City phone directory ... not beginning to end, anyway ... and not strictly speaking even through one volume.

I was going to read it on the train on the way from NYC to Providence, Rhode Island. I was told the US was a big country, which is why I chose a big book, but the train ran out of track before I ran out of As. Some big country — huh! Anyway I couldn't finish the phone directory on the way back to NYC because I was scheduled to read Proust's Memories of Things Past. I was going to read it backwards which seems the best way to approach memories. But you know how it is with long train rides. I'd got myself all psyched up and was about ready to get stuck into the book when we pulled up in Penn Station.

I have not read the Tibetan Book of the Dead.

I did read pi to three decimal places. Pi to three decimal places reads 3.142. The other day I inadvertently read the fourth decimal place which was 5. This meant the third place was not 2 after all, but 1 because 1 rounded up before a value larger than 4 is 2, which was kind of disappointing because it turned out I hadn't really read pi to three decimal places after all, only to two ... but there is some compensation in the fact that having read the fourth digit and been corrected on the third digit I am now two steps further on in an infinite series.

I have not read Mein Kampf.

I have, to my credit, read Marx's Capital — or as much of it as was necessary to scrape a pass in my political philosophy module at college, which is still more than most people have read of it and definitely more than your average Marxist, so I figure that counts as a full read.

September 02, 2003

Today I was in a plane crash.

Sausages for tea again.

August 29, 2003

Smokers. Don't you just hate them?

While I was waiting for my train this morning a smoker came up to me and without preamble called me a piece of shit, head butted me, kicked me in the balls, forced his fingers into my eyes and tried to throw me in front of a moving train.

But what really got me was the choking stink of cigarettes on him, like he had been chain smoking in a closet for a week. It made me want to gag. I really hate that.

August 28, 2003

Yesterday at the office I exploded. It was a big explosion and quite unexpected.

One minute I was proofing schedules — always a favourite activity — and the next minute, without any warning: boom — I was a mushroom cloud reaching right into the heavens, displacing the sky and showering fallout on everyone around me.

The fallout was the atomised remains of me. The dust of my spleen ended up in the boss's coffee — I hate coffee. My heart got mixed with the makeup on the pretty secretary's face and got into the pores of her skin. My lungs clogged the photocopier, my liver settled on the cactus and my hands and arms ended up embracing the world in a thin layer.

I don't think I endeared myself to my colleagues who were incinerated by the flash and demolished by the blast wave, but still, it was something different.

August 24, 2003

Surf: Gets clothes so clean it makes you want to masturbate!

August 22, 2003

An open letter to Certs, makers of breath mints.

Dear Certs,

Fuck you, I don't have bad breath.

Yours,

etc.

August 20, 2003

I met a speaking cat today. Imagine that: a cat that can speak! We talked at great length about a great many fascinating things. I had no idea a cat had such thoughts in its head.

A little cloudy today. Sausages for tea.

August 17, 2003

Inspiration is a cherry knocker.

August 16, 2003

A letter from my favourite uncle, who happens to live in the countryside, lucky so-and-so.

Dear nephew,

Every time he goes it's the same telephone city atrocity pain in the arse. Get over it. No way in no way out, running around the edge the concrete edge some big ruddy stone grey stone mausoleum jobbie landed by GOD right here, right out of the sky. Wolf whistle out of the blue blue blue with a very fucking sudden flatulent CRUMP. Farmer Shitpile, a man outstanding in his field in his own lunchtime never knew what hit him. But there it was. There it still is. We can plant around it but it ain't the same. No subsidy either. Out shooting rabbits — spotlights, jeeps. 12 bores, 12 good men this is true and a Bradley armoured fighting vehicle — found a load of them DRUIDS and DENTISTS wot moved out from the city DANCING round the bugger. Pan pipes, music, some without hats if you can believe that, rubber ducks stuck up their arses no doubt and all I shouldn't wonder think. Won't be trubblin us again.

Still there it is and there it was and the corn grows black around it and on warm nights the bats shun it and above it a sickle moon draws blood from the sky. No bloody subsidies. Lambs born dead a head at each end, turns crab apples into fisheries inspectors and the crows laugh. Could blame it on the nukes but I voted for them. I'm not daft. Hunt saboteurs are the best bet right now spoil it for everyone spongers never done a real day's. Care more about animals than people would murder us all in our porridge oats just to save a ruddy hedgehog. Reminds me, like my badger hat? I know you don't usually use the whole badger, but in this day and age it seems silly not to.

Keep well,

Unc. (Your favourite one, in the countryside)

Sausages for tea.

Star date df4.tger7.df4

Cars! Loads of them everywhere. Wherever you look: cars! Makes me think that maybe someone somewhere is making them. Thousands of them every week. Maybe they have a factory that churns these things out on huge production lines. And maybe someone — maybe even the same person that's making the cars — is making drivers too. Thousands, millions of drivers. As many drivers as there are cars in fact. One driver for each car! Imagine that. These drivers if they come off an assembly line are all identical: blank little stick men, which they bolt to the driver's seat. The workers point the cars out the factory gate, give them a push and off they go to run round and round the streets until they run out of gas or wear out or collide with something. Then the spent cars are taken to a yard and stacked high up, one on top of the other. I've seen the yards — piles of cars as far as the eye can see. But it has never occurred to me before that the drivers are inside.

January 23, 2003

Here's an interesting clipping from the local news section of today's paper.

Termites of Truth

There are towers over London, New York, Tokyo, Hong Kong, Singapore, Paris, Berlin ... Pure energy pointing right into the sky. The towers are flickering erratically like fluorescent tubes with faulty capacitors. They are like gods sustained by a collective act of faith. Even in these rational times, faith is an unlimited commodity. Rationality is faith and faith is an indefinitely large dirigible pig.

Yet questions will be asked despite an impressive array of prophylactic measures. Questions squeeze unbidden through the pores and the lines of our faces, between the classes at our schools and universities, from between words, through the sutures in our skulls. Questions like termites taking to the wind in summer, gathering in swarms and white clouds around lights or making for the moon. Men in noddy suits with tanks of insecticide on their backs feeding hoses, patrol and spray. The streets become thick carpets of dying, kicking insects but out of the black still they come. The Tokyo Metropolitan council at first denies responsibility, then recommends spraying the whole area from the air and gets on to the environment ministry since this is obviously their kind of job. Environment Ministry advises caution and an environmental impact study and since the termites are eating factories as well as homes the matter is passed to both the ministry of Surveys and the Ministry of Trade and Industry, who each, after long deliberations advise keeping an eye on the situation. The truth here is a matter that goes beyond issues of responsibility. The fact is, nobody has assigned a budget to deal with the problem and nobody wants to part with slices of their own pie when the Education Ministry is already doctoring text books to remove all mention of termites and generally tidy up the past to make a nice bed for the present.

In the end someone thinks to turn the tv on and we forget about the termites or the termites go away or the termites get on with their termiting or the termites get into watching tv too; it's hard to tell through all this laughter. And on the tv we can all see how we are getting on with the important things how we are getting on with building the Utopialand they've promised us for next week and which we can see all mocked up in computer graphics.

Fifty-storey trade centres on every street corner point right at the future: there it is, its foundations burrowed through a history that's ended up as a sea-reclamation project in the bay for another Portopia — engineers with megaphones line the shore and announce 'We've come back for our land.' Bailiffs tack eviction notices to the waves, the police wearing rubber rings line up behind them hopefully, and with a sigh the water parts. Council workmen go in first with sledgehammers and smash all the sea shells left behind and saw the legs off the sea bed to deny further use of them to anybody or anything. Then all the history excavated for the foundations of the future is dumped with lots of other used up junk into the space where the water used to be. On top of the junk we build towers with gaily coloured ironwork, we put fibreglass Goofeys, Minnies, Donalds, and especially Mickeys in the sculpted thirty-by-twenty natural parks with the skateboard ramps and the plastic ski slopes and we build a new airport to admit more money. And in the un-useful spaces we put un-useful people.

Sausages for tea.

October 31, 2002

Here's a letter to *The Times* by my favourite uncle (the other favourite uncle, not the one who lives in the countryside). He really is a clever fellow, don't you think?

Dear The Times,

With regard to your un-Timesly feature — carried not one Times, but two Times in your organ — 'Wriggling Embryos', which perchance refers to rumours of an unspecified but guessable event recently in the Far East somewhere, POINTED reference, I might add and will do, I the undersigned wish to nip in the bud.

I also want to draw your attention while Miller, aka Dusty, the valet shuffles on all fours under your desk and over to the whisky cabinet.

Reminds me of a chap I met in Salerno in '43. Had all his skin burned off by some ghastly Nazi prototype napalm, unless it was the Americans. Lay on the beach — more a pile of pebbles, really, and barbed wire — mewling 'Mummy! Mummy!' red as a side of beef, curled up with the stump of his hand in his mouth. 'Ah ha! You must be one of those lefties. Sod off and bleed to death slowly and agonisingly in someone else's war confusing issues like right and wrong, good and evil, Yorkshire pudding and bratwurst,' I said to him just after putting him out of his misery with a high heel through the temple. Oddest thing, his intestines escaped, snaked leaving a slimy trail of black congealing blood on the rocks, right between my legs and beyond where the fast draining tentacle found purchase in a nearby faceless cadaver, where nestled in the mouth of the red nova of face I got the idea of some kind of placenta, umbilical, foetus set up and scarpered to find a Hun on whom I could vent my excitement.

I ask: Where was the 'Wriggling Embryos' report back when we needed it, back at the dawn of creation? Don't give me that 'but our hacks were just amoeba' crap, what about responsibility to your profession? God damn it, man, a chap can't walk the streets without having embryos burrowing their way into manly, rugby ball gonads better otherwise employed. The Somme, Flanders, Ypres — now that was war, killing them off sixty thousand a day. That's the way to do it! That's the way to do it!

I contend the war made us all soft — reports of unbridled sexual indulgence in your press. YOUR press, God damn you! And this brings me to the quivering point of my ire: gross dereliction of FACT in your worthy journal. Or is it a cunning smokescreen to hide reality from the masses who have no business knowing at any rate. In case I am heaby blowing the gaff, I enclose a dotted line for you to snip along before publication to save you bother of arduous arduous censorship:

Wossallthisthen about the HMG's half brick and female

circumcision programme? Do you think we are all daft? That was discontinued a long time ago, yonks, to be precise, when the link up between Union Carbide, British Nuclear Fuels and Zanussi was achieved with the express purpose of solving the human problem by less laborious means. Porton Down was turned into a kiddies theme park not simply as a response to Delors' Euro-Disneyism but because the corporate alliance obviated the need for its existence. So there.

And that neatly brings me to the real point of this letter. I need advice, dear The Times. What can a chap do about the glacier-sized accretions of grey substance that persist behind my ears no matter how fastidious my valet is about personal hygiene? I have my head steam cleaned every evening, yet the next morning there the vile stuff is again, coming off on my fingers like grease from a kebab. Your reply is desperately awaited.

Yours,

Unc. (the other favourite one, not the one in the countryside)

Day one

July 28th, 2001

I came across a remarkable pebble today. Quite by chance.

Sausages for tea.